Dedication:

This book is dedicated to all at Whi Reenactment Group, Without them, this book would not be possible and without the Town itself wouldn't be possible to have the amazing community that we have. A special thanks to Tony whose dream wouldn't have been reality if it wasn't for Tom.

About The Author:

My Name is Andy. M Chapman, and I've been a western re-enactor for nearly 30 years now, My fascination in history started as a young boy like many children visiting museums and castles and enjoying history lessons during my school years. We all enjoyed playing with toy soldiers or cowboys & Indians as children, our imagination ran wild, and for some of us I guess we didn't want to grow up.

I began my re-enactment years as portraying American WW2 soldier and was about a join a local group, An old friend introduced me to a earlier period of the American West, So I joined their group instead, I portrayed a US cavalry man during the 1870's (Indian Wars), After many years of living history shows and events, I was asked if I would like to join Whiteoak Springs re-enactment group, which I did in 2019

I started to write short stories for the Whiteoak Springs Town Gazette just to help with raising money for the town funds, people who enjoyed the stories suggested that I would publish them so here we are!

Prologue:

This is a fictional place built on a farm in Derbyshire, it is called Stenson Hill farm, Stenson Fields, All the buildings have been built by the town members over the past few years, their interest in the American West during the 1800's.

'Whiteoak Springs' is a remarkable frontier town of the west, Built to a captivating charm, its history would take you back to the wild west of the 1800s, this town is treasured destination for both history enthusiasts and reenactors alike. Its picturesque streets are lined with beautifully built buildings, each one telling a unique story of the folks that thrive here. As you wander through the town, you'll be transported back in time, awed by the authentic architecture and the palpable sense of the Wild West. From the Old Saloon, where locals and guests can gather for lively conversations and poker games, and listen to music of the time, then on to the General Store that provides nostalgic goods, and on every corner of Whiteoak Springs is a pioneering spirit. With its vibrant community and an annual round-up that celebrates the town's heritage every July, there's always an opportunity to immerse yourself in the lively atmosphere. Whiteoak Springs offers an unforgettable experience that will transport you back in time. The wild west rugged terrain is a playground for the brave and the bold, enticing you to push your limits, to embrace the thrill of the unknown. Whiteoak's is a place where the spirit of adventure thrives, where new discoveries and the untamed awaits those who dare to explore. So, strap on your boots, don your hat, and get ready to embark on a wild west adventure like no other, where the rugged terrain becomes the backdrop to your own tales of daring and discovery, Welcome to Whiteoak Springs Western Town...............

Contents:

Chapter 1 – Introduction!

Chapter 2 - Meet the Town's People

The Short Stories ....

Chapter 3 – In the Beginning!

Chapter 4 - The Ladies of Whiteoak's (Temperance Society)

Chapter 5 – Walk with The Marshal

Chapter 6 – Deputy Tate

Chapter 7 - 13 Miles to Whiteoak's

Chapter 8 – A Map Maker's Tale

Chapter 9 – English Jack

Chapter 10 - Ms Kitty's Downfall

Chapter 11 – A New Day

Chapter 12 – The Hunt for English Jack

Chapter 13 – Who Shot Bubba? (The Town Mayor)

Chapter 14 - The Siege Of Whiteoak's

Chapter 15 - Acknowledgements

Chapter 1

Introduction:

In 2017 Mr Whiteoak (Tony) A former lorry driver and Western reenactor worked for Mr Atwal (Tom) landowner and businessman, as Toms Estates manager, Marie, Tony's partner helps run the livery and horses, She owned horses herself, and has experience running yards, After a time Toms and Tony's friendship grew, There was a dis-used Avery, and an old small petting zoo was in disrepair. As this was an old attraction for the Holiday homes that Mr Atwal rents out, Mr Atwal (Tom) asked Tony what he would do with the small parcel of Land, Tony replied, I would build a western town that has been my ultimate dream. Tom turned around and gave Tony the go ahead. As time went on their friendship grew, Tony converted the old petting zoo into a large cabin and then started to ask friends if they would come and be a part of the project and build, he then had 3 to 4 cabins not quite a town but certainly taking shape. From just a small few cabins' rising to a thriving town as it is today.

I joined 2019, although I was invited at the start I wasn't in a position to build at the time, By this time the town was thriving and expanding and in 2022 saw its 5th year anniversary and it has progressed into an impressive sight with every Cabin, Store, Saloon, Offices and buildings very much like an old frontier western town should be, It is an area that western re-enactors can camp in authentic setting, There is lots a hard work and a community spirit to help each other, many of us with great knowledge of history of the West. This is Whiteoak Springs Western Town reenactment group, Each one is unique, and everyone has their part to play on round ups and public visits. People who have visited couldn't believe the amount of detail that has been put into the town, also it's been used for professional photography and video shoots. But still in its infant stages, I'm sure and along with its community it will mature.

My Role is the US Marshal a lawman, but I also write a fictional News Paper called Whiteoak Springs Gazette, Where I write and print monthly stories based on fact and fiction. Fact is taken from real newspaper archives using Texas Digital Newspaper Program and fiction is what the good town folk get up to at the weekend on our roundups.

I have been a western re-enactor for many years like most of our members and part of this book is based on short Stories with our town's characters in the fictional town of Whiteoak's and of the newspaper writing of the fictional County of Stenson which is loosely based in Texas.

Chapter 2

Meet the Town's People:

An Introduction to the re-enactors who have built the town and a series of short stories based on the characters of the town from Skits/Sketches they acted out during round ups.

Meet the town's people, Each owning their own abode, Their real names, and their town characters they portray, They all have a unique fictional background in the enchanting world of Whiteoak's, each person has their own captivating story and unique role to fulfil. Amongst the colourful tapestry of characters, a sprinkle of fictional figures adds an extra dash of excitement. While their back stories may primarily be works of imagination, they add an intriguing layer to the narrative. It is in this realm that the adventurous spirit truly comes alive, as individuals embrace their extraordinary journeys within the realms of Whiteoak's. Whether soaring through undiscovered lands, unravelling mysteries, or facing unimaginable danger, every character plays their part with unyielding determination and a thirst for discovery. Within the enchanting pages of this book, you will see the thrilling tone of adventure pulsates, inviting readers to join in on this wondrous journey.

No 1 Main Street - Sheriff Office – Mr Mark Smith (Trooper Smiff/Sheriff) Mrs Shelly Smith (Mrs Smiff)

Sheriff Smiff, a larger-than-life character with a colourful background and a knack for unintentional clumsiness, is a humorous force to be reckoned with in the West. Picture a burly man donning a perfectly pressed, albeit crooked, cowboy hat that seems to have a mind of its own. With a quick wit and a knack for snappy comebacks, Sheriff Smiff has the uncanny ability to turn any situation into a comical spectacle. Whether he's tripping over his own spurs or fumbling to draw his trusty six-shooter, his bumbling nature never fails to draw laughter and muffled chuckles from the townsfolk. Unbeknownst to him, his enthusiasm and sheer obliviousness to his own mishaps only add to his endearing charm.

Sheriff Smiff story starts as Trooper Smiff born in the County of Kent England, around 1825 the son of a house painter. At 10 years old apprenticed to a local charcoal burner and bodger he was preparing lunch when a spark set fire to the thatch of the Manor House, they were working but the place burnt to the ground. In fear of his life Trooper ran to the port of Chatham hoping to jump a ship and escape the wrath of his master. However short of money he was talked into joining the Army as a drummer boy. He was found to have a natural way with horses when as appointed groom to his commander this was in 1843, he was offered the chance to join the 14th Hussars who were about to be posted for service in India. It was while serving that he adapted the name Trooper as his given name of Agamemnon was too hard for his corporal to spell on the muster roll. However, Trooper fell into debt with several of his comrades from being bad at cards and again in fear of his life took the chance to jump ship onto an American whaler when his ship's Captain came too in mid ocean to obtain fresh water from another whaling ship. Now a deserter Trooper Smiff arrived in New York in 1849 and took work in a coach builders' workshop. Trooper stayed in this job for almost 8 years raising to the position of head sweeper and greaser. One day Trooper was tasked to grease the carriage of the Mayor of New York but didn't notice grease had spilled onto the mounting step. Later that evening the mayor summoned his carriage, stood on to the step, slipped banging his chin, screamed in pain which scared the horses who jumped forward pulling the carriage wheels ran over his foot, instantly breaking his foot. Again, in fear of his life Trooper took off. Travelling around the nation from job to job. Arriving in Texas in 1859 and gaining work in a livery stable near Fort Worth. At the onset of the war of northern aggression he enlisted in the 8th Texas Cavalry.

At war's end he returned to the livery where he met his now wife Michelle known as Shelly, whose father kept two horses at the livery. Once married, Trooper saw an opportunity in ranching in the growing cattle business feeding the big cities back East. Gangs of rustlers and bandits roamed the South, but the law was short on the ground, Trooper was sick of seeing his cows stolen he traded his branding iron for a badge and became a deputy Sheriff in Waco. Serving with some distinction he was mentioned by a district Judge to Marshall Chapman of Whiteoak Springs as a candidate for Deputy Marshal, Trooper Smiff was elected as Deputy and he and Shelly moved to Whiteoak Springs in 73. But later, Deputy Marshal Smiff stepped down as Deputy Marshal and took the position of Town Sheriff as Whiteoak springs had grown and needed its own town Sheriff, he was elected over the Easter weekend in 75 after two years helping out as Deputy Marshal.

The Marshal and Smiff made good ground by keeping the peace. U.S. Marshals generally deal with federal appointments and normally deal with outlaws who broke federal laws, but also doubled up as peace officers within the town's limits alongside the Sheriff. It was time for the newly appointed Sheriff to make his own mark on the town. Marshal Chapman wasn't far away if he needed help and by the time he was elected Two Rangers had been appointed a small office just on the outskirts of Whiteoak's to help keep the peace.

On one particular day Sheriff Smiff, known for his wits and cunning, found himself in a rather extraordinary predicament. In a stunning turn of events, he was utterly bamboozled by a precocious young girl, who, with the help of her daring companion Henry McCarty, managed to stage a daring jailbreak right under his nose. Adding to the chaos, notorious bandit Antonio seized the opportunity to make his escape alongside them. leaving Sheriff Smiff scratching his head in disbelief. No doubt, this unexpected turn of events provided a comedic twist to an otherwise ordinary day in the chaotic life of a sheriff. the Marshal had been tirelessly tracking Antonio for months, his determination fuelled by a mix of disbelief and frustration that the notorious criminal had managed to escape jail. Despite the numerous close calls and dead ends, Marshal remained calm, Marshal Chapman had commented on the situation as it left a sour note in the air, but the Sheriff couldn't apologise more for embarrassment and took the Marshal to lunch to explain the events.

Turns out that Henry McCarty would later be the infamous 'Billy the Kid'. Well, that one is for the real history books. The 'Gazette' wrote: He was quite embarrassed, As two outlaws escaped from his newly furnished Jail, Henry McCarty a youngster picked up for a minor affray and Bandit Antonio had given the Sheriff the slip, the pair had dupped the sheriff with the aid of a young girl believed to be travelling with Henry McCarty. When it came to sorting out disputes, the Sheriff was like a human magnet for mayhem. It seemed like folks in town couldn't go a day without calling on his wisdom and wit to untangle their messes. Whether it was rowdy bar brawls, heated arguments over property lines, or even who saw the squirrel first, the Sheriff never failed to bring his A-game to the table. With a quick wit and an uncanny ability to see through the fog of confusion, he had a knack for diffusing tension with a well-timed joke or a clever remark. It was almost as if he had a sixth sense for keeping the peace, and the townsfolk adored him for it. From dawn till dusk, the Sheriff can be seen strolling the streets, settling squabbles with his light-hearted banter and a twinkle in his eye, The day he gracefully slipped across the walkway like a dancer, only to unexpectedly land smack in the middle of a fire bucket was undeniably comical. Resting on his backside in a puddle of water But alas, amusement was a privilege only bestowed upon the onlookers, for he found himself submerged in a watery abyss. Oh, what a sight it must have been; a spectacle that elicited laughter until tears streamed down rosy cheeks. However, despite the embarrassing mishap, there was something ineffable about him that made it impossible not to warm up to him.

The day were he decided to put on his belt but completely forgot about strapping on his trusty pistol. As he sauntered around, feeling like a real fashionista with his belt cinched just right, he couldn't help but wonder why he felt strangely incomplete. Perhaps it was the empty holster dangling by his side, mocking him for his absent-mindedness. The Sheriff's laugh is something truly infectious. Picture this: a boisterous, jovial sound escaping from his lips, contagious enough to make even the sternest of outlaws crack a smile. With each hearty chuckle, the room comes alive, as if basking in the warmth of his delightful amusement. It's a laugh that carries the essence of his personality, as he effortlessly blends quick-witted jokes with a dash of playful banter.

No 2 Main Street - Brokenwood Mercantile – Ms Kate Mason (Ms Kate, Shop keeper) Mr Phil Powling (Bubba Western, Town Mayor)

Bubba

Ms Kate

Welcome to Brokenwood Mercantile, where Bubba and Kate run the show with their warm and friendly spirits! This charming little shop nestled in the heart of Whiteoak's offers a delightful assortment of goods that are sure to catch your eye. As you step inside, you'll be greeted with a genuine smile and a heartfelt "howdy" from Bubba and Kate, who always make it their mission to ensure a pleasant shopping experience for everyone who walks through their doors. From locally sourced produce and handcrafted wares to household treasures and quirky curiosities, they have carefully curated a collection that caters to the diverse tastes of their loyal customers. Their infectious enthusiasm and personal touch create a welcoming atmosphere that is hard to resist. Whether you're a regular or a first-time visitor, be prepared for a delightful shopping adventure at Brokenwood Mercantile, where Bubba and Kate's friendly demeanour will make you feel right at home.

Bubba a young man born in Kentucky with no surviving family. He was moving from town to town looking for stable employment as war broke out. Bubba enlisted into the confederacy as a regular infantryman for the 4th Kentucky Bubba survived the first encounter the battle of Shiloh in April 1862, were his regiment lost nearly half of its men then went on throughout the war toward the end 4th Kentucky was then ordered to Griffin, Georgia and converted to mounted infantry. The regiment engaged in delaying tactics during Sherman's March to the Sea, following him all the way to Savannah, Georgia, finally moving to Augusta, Georgia, in early 1865. His last engagement was on April 29, 1865, in a skirmish near Stateburg, South Carolina. At the close of the war, the 4th Kentucky was ordered to Washington, Georgia and surrendered on May 7, 1865. Bubba was left with nowhere to go, One of his compatriots and companion decided to set up as travelling salesmen unfortunately for Bubba he was robbed and hurt near Georgia, Aimlessly wondering south he meet up with a young lady named Kate, Kate also suffered as a Mormon she had run away from her husband who had taken several wives and feared of being hunted and sent back. The Mormons Controversy opposition by the United States government and immoral behaviour with young girls saw President Grant's administration prosecute Mormon polygamists, and vice crimes like pornography, and abortion. The pair moved south towards Texas on their way selling small tin items and other goods to travellers as they passed, By the time they entered Whiteoak's they decided to settle together and build and open the General Store Known as 'Brokenwood' the store got its name from its humble beginnings, Once a shack strengthened by steel railroad rods, Governor Atwal insisted on the building should be built more traditionally, it took 10 men to take down the original shack hence 'Brokenwood' and the general store was born.

No 4 Main Street - R&R Fur Traders Mrs Sue Hancock (Storekeeper/Baker) Mr Neil Hancock (Red Fur Trapper) Mr Ben Hancock (Reno, Fur Trapper)

Red   **Sue**   **Reno**

R&R Fur Traders, a family-owned business, consists of Sue, the storekeeper/baker, her husband Red, a seasoned fur trapper, and their son Reno, who is following in his father's footsteps. With their warm and welcoming nature, this friendly family has become a pillar of their community. Sue greets customers with her infectious smile and offers delectable treats from her bakery, ensuring everyone feels at home when they step into their store. Meanwhile, Red's extensive knowledge of fur trapping and his genuine interest in helping others have earned him the respect and admiration of fellow trappers. The apple doesn't fall far from the tree, as Reno embodies his parents' friendliness and enthusiasm. Always ready to lend a hand or share stories of his trapping adventures, Reno has become the go-to fur trapper for both advice and companionship. Overall, the R&R Fur Traders are not only known for their exceptional products but for being the kind of people who brighten your day with their warm personalities.

R&R fur traders has been running for generations with the original members moving from England to work for the Hudson Bay fur trade A royal charter from King Charles II incorporated "The Governor and Company of Adventurers of England, trading into Hudson's Bay" on 2 May 1670. The charter granted the company a monopoly over the region drained by all rivers and streams flowing into Hudson Bay in northern parts of present-day Canada. The area was named

"Rupert's Land" after Prince Rupert, the first governor of the company appointed by the King. HBC established six posts between 1668 and 1717. Rupert House (1668, southeast), Moose Factory (1673, south) and Fort Albany, Ontario (1679, west) were erected on James Bay; three other posts were established on the western shore of Hudson Bay New Severn (1685) York Factory (1684) and Fort Churchill (1717). Inland posts were not built until 1774. After 1774, York Factory became the main post because of its convenient access to the vast interior waterway-systems of the Saskatchewan and Red rivers. Originally called "factories" because the "factor", i.e., a person acting as a mercantile agent, did their business from there, these posts operated in the manner of the Dutch fur-trading operations in New Netherland. By adoption of the Standard of Trade.

The family continued to work for the company through the ages until the HBC relinquished control of the land to Canada in 1869 as part of the Deed of Surrender, authorized by the Rupert's Land Act 1868, By this time Red and Sue and a young Reno moved into the States looking for an opportunity to set up a trading post, with a wealth of family knowledge soon traded fine pelts from state to state, finally they reached Whiteoak springs were they decided to set a small trading post as Red and Sue wanting to settle but young Reno had developed into a fine trader and trapper with collecting many fine pelts from across the country selling high end pelts. Reno grew with his knowledge of the way of the Indian and found it easy to trade. You can find the trading post along Main Street of Whiteoak's. Sue joined the Temperance Society where she makes cakes to raise monies and helps to organise the societies' function.

No 5 Main Street Boxx & Co land Registry & Assay Office Mr John Edwards (John Boxx Registrar and Assay) Ms Joanna Rowe (Lady Eva Fouquet Assay Office)

Mr J Boxx

Allow me to introduce you to two remarkable individuals who play crucial roles at the Registry & Assay Office. Meet Mr. John Boxx, the charismatic character known for his exceptional dedication to his work. His warm smile and friendly demeanour, Miss Eva Fouquet, the extraordinary talented person, with her approachable and affable nature, Makes even the most intricate procedures appear effortless with her attention to detail.

John story begins, Born in 1830 in Staffordshire, John R Edwards was the son of Terrence and Dorothy Edwards. Terrence was a skilled worker in the Staffordshire pottery industry and worked closely with 3 brothers, Daniel, Edwin, and William Bennet. The 3 brothers, originally from Darbyshire, also had an older brother James who in 1835 had emigrated to America and was now thriving in his own pottery venture in the small town of East Liverpool, Ohio. James in fact was doing so well that in 1841 he sent word back to England and requested for his brothers to join him to run the expanding business. The 3 brothers agreed to join James on the condition that they could bring Terrence with them. They had worked a long time with Terrance and knew his potential to be a great potter and believed he would be a great asset to the company, "The Bennett and Brothers Pottery Company". So, in September 1841 when Terrence was offered the chance to emigrate to America, his whole family jumped at the chance and moved to East Liverpool, which had a population of only 500 people. John grew up in a loving wholesome family, in this quiet little town, John though was not a "quiet lifestyle" kind of guy and wanted to make a name for himself, so in his late teens he started looking west for a more exciting life. After a period of traveling and exploring, John put down roots in Lincoln County,

New Mexico, which was a bustling, energetic town with no shortage of drama, After a short while, John was offered the position of Sheriff due to his big personality. and authoritative nature and took to his new role like a duck to water, in fact it suited him so well that again he needed "more" and started bending the rules to his benefit and gain and was known to be slightly corrupt and a person you didn't want to get on the wrong side of, but it was generally accepted by most as he did do a good job (in a fashion) of keeping law and order. As Lincoln town's population grew and grew, John's tactics for keeping order sometimes got him into a spot of bother as people coming to the town would often challenge his position and John wasn't shy of standing his ground.

But in 1858 John met a young Lady Named Miss Eva Fouquet who was passing through town with her traveling band, and the pair became inseparable. So much so that when the band were ready to move further west, Eva stayed behind to make a life with John. A couple of years, and children later, Eva was getting increasingly worried that John's role in Lincoln county would be the death of him and urged him to step down as sheriff and find a more relaxed lifestyle. John too had been considering his future and often thought he may prematurely end up in a box in the ground so confided in his longtime friend Josey Wales, who was the Marshal in a small up and coming town called Whiteoak springs. Josey urged John to join him at Whiteoak's and after a word with the governor, Josey offered John the role of Proprietor of the land Registry for this peaceful expanding town. John Eva and family packed up and headed to Whiteoak springs and opened the town's first official land registry "boXx and Company". John, Now known as BoXx became a prominent person in the town helping to develop it further and left behind his previous devious ways and settled into a more respectable role. Due to his previous bad ways, BoXx was slightly paranoid that one day maybe someone from his past would catch up with him wanting revenge, so he always kept many lamps lit (some debated too many!) so he could see anyone approaching and he could never be caught off guard.

Miss Eva Fouquet was born in 1838 in Staffordshire to a prominent family. Her mother was an entrepreneurial business lady dabbling her hand in many pots, and her father was a leading rubber exporter between Britain and the New York commission house. Due to the development of vulcanized rubber in 1839, and the boom that followed, Eva and her family ended up emigrating permanently to America. Her father became the British ambassador for Goodyear based in America.

Lady Eva Fouquet

Young Eva grew up in a stable loving environment and had a happy childhood but was always surrounded by business motivated people and she found herself wanting to be a little more creative. She was a strong-willed young lady and going against her parents' wishes, in her late teens, she began performing in the New York bars as a singer and made quite a name for herself. Further to this, she then joined a band of musicians so she could experience more, and they too had great success along the east coast.

When Eva was in her early 20's the band decided to head west looking for more excitement after hearing stories of the gold rush but by the time they had reached Lincoln County Eva was fed up with traveling the long, hard days and nights and was looking for something more suitable for the independent young lady she had become. It was while in Lincoln County that she met John R Edwards, the local sheriff, and they became closely acquainted. John was known as having a ruthless reputation so when Eva informed her mother that she was leaving the band and staying in Lincoln with John her mother was not too pleased, but when the band left Eva stayed behind anyway. Eva and John settled in Lincoln, and it was only after they'd had a couple of children that they decided to look at moving to a more peaceful environment as John's job could often bring trouble to the door. An opportunity arose in an up-and-coming town called Whiteoak springs, so they packed up and moved. It was while in Whiteoak's that Eva decided she would like to open an Assay office and with her upbringing in a business-oriented family she was fully suited to this position. She opened her office next door to the land registry that was now operated by John and together they became BoXx & Company. Eva fully immersed herself in town life. She worked very hard and would have a go and help at anything that would help to develop or benefit the town. Every now and then she would even perform in the town saloon.

No 6 Main Street Barbers Shop Mr Franco Onorati (Franco, Barber/Gunman/Cowhand) Mrs Filomena Onorati (Filomena, Barbers Wife)

Franco and his wife Filomena run a delightful barbershop that radiates warmth and camaraderie. From the moment you step through the door, you can feel the friendly atmosphere enveloping you like a familiar hug. Smiles and genuine conversations flow effortlessly between the patrons and the couple, creating a sense of belonging that is unmatched. Franco's skilled hands and attention to detail result in impeccable haircuts, while Filomena's infectious laughter and warm personality put everyone at ease. Franco and Filomena's dedication to providing exceptional service goes beyond just styling hair; they go the extra mile to make everyone feel like family. Whether it's exchanging stories or offering a listening ear, their barbershop isn't just a place to look good but a sanctuary where lifelong friendships are forged. Like many Europeans Franco and his wife Filomena arrived in New York from Italy to find their wealth and fortune they arrived in the mid-50s and settled near Toms River New Jersey. New York has its problems like many other cities Infectious diseases, such as cholera, tuberculosis, typhus, and malaria and yellow fever, had plagued New York City along with Slums and Gangs was such a dangerous place to be. Residents took advantage of the disorganized state of the city's police force, brought about by the conflict between the Municipal and Metropolitan police, gangsters, and other criminals from all parts of the city began to engage in widespread looting and the destruction of property. The Daily National Intelligencer of July 8th 57 estimated that between 800 and 1,000 gang members took part in the riots, along with several hundred others who used the disturbance to loot the Bowery area. It was the largest disturbance since the Astor Place Riot in 49. Order was restored by the New York State Militia (under Major-General Charles W. Sandford), supported by detachments of city police. Eight people were reported killed, and more than 100 people received serious injuries.

As war broke, Franco and Filomena tried to stay neutral but as many Italian Americans joined the Union Army and were recruited from New York City. Franco joined the 39th New York Volunteer Infantry Regiment, under Giuseppe Garibaldi. The unit wore red shirts and bersaglieri plumes. They carried with them both a Union Flag as well as an Italian flag with the words Dio e popolo, meaning "God and people". Surviving the war Franco was living in a slum and fearing for their lives they left New York travelling westward with the large migrations, and picking up odd jobs along their way, Their hope was to find their way to New Jersey and the vineyards of California, but with the eccentric trend setters in the cities and fashions coming from Paris a large number of barber shops started to open up. Franco and his wife saw the opportunity to make a living from this and finally settling in Whiteoak's in 73 they found the opportunity to have their very own Barber's Shop in the Frontier town. This is due to open soon situated on main street near the Painted Pony Saloon.

No 8 Main Street Apothecary Mr Ian Lyle (Jeb, Cartographer) Mrs Kath Lyle (Olive, Herbalist)

Jeb **Olive**

The Apothecary, owned and run by the dynamic duo of Jeb, a seasoned cartographer and illustrator, and Olive, a skilled herbalist. This charming little establishment is bursting with an inviting atmosphere and a warm sense of hospitality.

As you enter, you'll be greeted by the comforting aroma of dried herbs and fragrant botanicals that line the shelves. Jeb and Olive, with their constant smiles and friendly demeanour, are always ready to share their extensive knowledge on the healing properties of each herb and guide you towards the remedies that best suit your needs.

Be it a common cold or a troubled mind, they're dedicated to helping their customers find natural and effective solutions. The apothecary is not just a place to purchase remedies, but also a sanctuary for indulging in conversations about travels, nature, and ancient healing practices. Jeb and Olive's passion for their craft shines through in every interaction, making your visit to their apothecary a delightful and enriching experience.

Jeb & Olive of the Apothecary, Olive being an herbalist studied botany and schooled in England later moving back to New Hampshire to her father's chemist and druggist's store, She helped out all hours her father being widowed when olive was young. Between them they ran the store, But as war broke out the father enlisted as surgeon and never returned. leaving Olive with the store and debts. Jeb a young adventure and amateur cartographer was son of an Anglo German army officer who fought in the Franco-Prussian War, Jeb was employed by the Nation Geographic on an exhibition to help map parts of South America particularly Peru.

Jeb arrived back in the States after a couple of years as the war was ending, and he was looking for a passage back to England then onto Europe. while waiting in New York for his advancement from the Nation Geographic he was invited by another young fellow cartographer in New Hampshire wishing to map out parts of the Northwest Territories, Having already returned from a dangerous perilous environment he declined, Just by chance he met Olive, and both having English connections and education the pair decided to move south, and they found haven in the frontier Town of Whiteoak's setting up a small and prosperous Apothecary, Where Olive used her herbal knowledge and chemist skills making cures, lotions and tonics , while Jeb worked for the Southern Railroad Surveying then later on mapping out the Town with the backing from the Governor.

No 9 Main Street Thomas Trust & Saving Bank Mr Dave Thomas (Mr Thomas Bank Manager/Pickerton) Mrs Caroline Thomas (Mrs P Bankers Wife/Retired Baker)

Meet Mr Thomas, a seasoned banker and owner, and his charming wife Mrs P, they are from a small town called Grantham in England travelled to New York in the early 30s before heading to Atlanta. They stayed in the city before the war, Where Mrs P opened a small bakery, Business was flourishing selling biscuits and Gravy to the needy, and supplying other baked goods throughout the community, As war broke out and Atlanta became a nexus of multiple railroads which made the city a strategic hub for the distribution of military supplies, Mrs P saw the this to be an opportunity to make hardtack for the troops. Mr Thomas joined the militia and rode with a small band of men during the war and Mrs P continued to bake. In 64 he returned to the city only to find that the city was evacuated and most of its public buildings had been destroyed, General Sherman prepared for the Union Army's March to the Sea by ordering the destruction of Atlanta's remaining military assets. Mr Thomas was unable to locate Mrs P so he rode back out to find her. He finally found a small encampment of refugees and there was Mrs P baking Biscuits & Gravy under a small canvas tarp. The couple moved on and headed south. Mr Thomas saw an opportunity to sell stocks and bonds making a small success of this, Mrs P continued to bake, they finally saw an opening at Whiteoak's to open a bank, 'Thomas Trust and Savings'. As the bank proprietor Mr Thomas managed to forage alliances through major cities in the banking world. Dealing with bonds, stocks and shares and sometimes land, he precured a successful bank where many of Whiteoak's folk trust their hard earnt cash, now insured against robbery he was soon approached by the Pinkerton Detective agency to help with the small office in Whiteoak's as they provide security for the bank and mine. Mr Thomas is a well-respected gentleman throughout Stenson territory. Mrs P has now retired from baking but helps the needy from time to time at Whiteoak's with her infamous biscuits and gravy.

After decades of dedicated service as a cook and bank cashier, Mrs Thomas (affectionately known as Mrs P) decided to retire and embrace a more leisurely lifestyle occasionally helping out as the Town cashier. Their lives now exude relaxation, as they revel in the tranquillity of their well-deserved break. Mr Thomas effortlessly switches gears from managing his banking endeavours to basking in the joys of ownership, while Mrs P finds solace in the memories of her culinary adventures and is a part of the temperance society. Unfortunately, the bank has undeniably transformed into a relentless magnet for outlaws. It seems that these nefarious individuals view the institution as a prime opportunity to exploit and wreak havoc on innocent civilians and their hard-earned assets. With audacity and cunning, they have made it their mission to breach the bank's defences and plunder its wealth. This audacious behaviour, undeterred by the consequences of their actions, necessitates an unwavering commitment from the authorities to protect the sanctity of Whiteoak's financial institution. Mr. Thomas, recognizing the importance of safeguarding the bank's assets, took a decisive step by appointing a Pinkerton detective. This strategic move aimed to heighten security on days when the bank receives large sums of money or during the transportation of silver. By enlisting the expertise of a Pinkerton detective, a renowned agency known for its professionalism and effectiveness, Mr. Thomas displayed a strong commitment to protecting the bank's valuables and ensuring customer trust. The Pinkerton detective, known as "Lawdog," comes equipped with a wealth of extensive training and experience in the field. With a steadfast commitment to upholding the law, "Lawdog" upholds the values and professionalism that the Pinkerton agency embodies. With a meticulous attention to detail, sharp instincts, and a well-honed skillset, "Lawdog" stands as an imposing force for justice. Over the span of six years, the Bank at Whiteoak's has unfortunately become the target of numerous acts of robbery, with at least seven or eight incidents reported. Undoubtedly, these recurrent events have presented substantial challenges for the bank's future. For Lawmen, such as Marshal Chapman and Sheriff Smith, dealing with the aftermath of these robberies has undoubtedly proven to be a recurring headache. Despite their best efforts to address and prevent such incidents, the persistence of these unfortunate events demands an unwavering commitment to preserving the safety and security of the bank's premises and its valued customers. It is not uncommon for robbers to flee empty-handed, leaving dedicated lawmen like Marshal Chapman and Sheriff Smiff to diligently pursue justice. Although the majority of the time these criminals escape with nothing, this does not deter these law enforcement officials from their mission to apprehend them and serve Justice. The bank in our town is not just a place to make deposits and withdrawals; it's also a vibrant hub for the community to come together and socialize. Amidst the bustling atmosphere of people taking care of their financial transactions, you'll often find friends and neighbours engaged in cheerful conversations. It's a place where stories are shared, laughter echoes through the walls, and deep-rooted connections are fostered, Mr & Mrs Thomas greet everyone with warm smiles and lend a listening ear to the triumphs and challenges of their customers. Whether it's a quick catch-up with an old acquaintance or a chance encounter with a new friend, the bank serves as a social epicentre, creating a sense of togetherness in our close-knit community.

No 10 Main Street School house Ms Jackie Mansell (Dolly School Teacher)

Ms Dolly

Ms. Dolly is the epitome of a warm and welcoming schoolteacher at Whiteoak's. With her friendly demeanour and genuine smile, she effortlessly creates a positive and inclusive learning environment for her children that attend. Ms. Dolly's passion for teaching shines through in her ability to connect with each child on a personal level, making them feel valued and heard. Whether she's patiently explaining a difficult concept or encouraging the children to think critically, Ms. Dolly's dedication to their success is evident in her every interaction. Beyond academics, she encourages the children to embrace kindness and respect, fostering a sense of community within the classroom. In Ms. Dolly's class, learning is not only about textbooks and assignments, but also about personal growth and building relationships.

Ms Dolly was born a raised in Lincoln County, She wanted to be educated and wanting to see young children to have an education too. Her family was deprived of this and was unable to send her to school, but a local prostitute schooled her to a degree of high education while doing jobs for her family. Many children on the frontier helped with the cooking, cleaning, mending, gathering eggs, and taking care of the younger children also keeping the fire going, fetching water, and caring for livestock. Boys helped with the planting and harvesting of crops and helped hunt for food to feed the family, some children even worked outside the home to make extra money for their families. Ms Dolly's life wasn't dissimilar, In the early 1870s, two men by the names of Lawrence Murphy and James Dolan owned the only store in Lincoln County – Murphy & Dolan Mercantile and Banking. Soon, another man named John Riley also entered the business. At the time, Lincoln County was the largest county in the nation, covering 1/5 of New Mexico territory. In addition to the store, Murphy & Dolan also owned large cattle ranches. Before long, Murphy & Dolan Mercantile and Banking monopolized the trade of the county, controlling pricing, making immense profits on their goods, and virtually having a hand in nearly every part of the economy of the large county. The merchants, along with their allies, which included local law enforcement, were familiarly known as "The House." For obvious reasons, Murphy and his allies were disliked by the small farmers and ranchers in Lincoln County as they were forced to pay high costs for their goods, while at the same time, accepting low prices for their cattle, Ms Dolly wanted to move away from all this which was causing much hardship. She found Whiteoak's as a safe haven and set up a small school building where she now teaches the young after they have done their chores. The schoolhouse in a long Main Street and you often see young children about enjoying themselves.

No 11 Main Street Gunsmiths Mr Tony Whiteoak (Josey Wales Gunsmith) Ms Marie Williams (Marie Horse Trader/Dealer)

Let me introduce you to the delightful duo of Mr. Whiteoak, the talented gunsmith, and Ms. Marie, the skilled horse dealer. These two individuals embody warmth and camaraderie in their shared passion for their respective trades. Mr. Whiteoak's expertise in crafting and repairing firearms is surpassed only by his amiable nature, making every customer feel like a cherished friend. Meanwhile, Ms. Marie's knowledge and love for horses shine through in her work, as she matches each rider with their perfect equine companion. Their friendly demeanour and genuine enthusiasm create a welcoming atmosphere where customers are not just clients, but part of a close-knit community. In the hands of Mr. Whiteoak and Ms. Marie, the worlds of guns and horses become not just businesses, but places of friendship and shared interests, fostering connections and fostering a true sense of belonging.

Mr Whiteoak was one of the first settlers of Whiteoak's alongside the Governor Mr T Atwal he has establish and contributed immensely to the town and has seen it grow from its humble beginnings to what it is today. Little is known about Mr Whiteoak in his early years, rumours said he was a drifter, ranch hand or a farmer, but he did serve for the Confederacy and some reported that he rode with 'Bloody Bill Anderson' as a partisan raider and was involved in many fights raiding supply lines and observation posts throughout Missouri, In fear of being captured towards the end of the war, it is believed he wintered in Texas and decided to stay while others went back to find their demise. Many from Whiteoak's dismiss this and since the war he is often mistaken for a well-known outlaw with many bounty hunters turning up to Whiteoak's from time to time who are widely disappointed to find a humble Mr Whiteoak. I must add that an outlaw is still believed to be on the run from federal government said to have visited Whiteoak's back in November last as the Marshal was questioned by Federal Troops at the time and the outlaw in question believed to have ridden with 43rd Virginia Cavalry 'Mosby's Rangers' and was one of the last units to surrender. Mr Whiteoak is the proprietor of the Gunsmiths No1 Main Street, and which was one of the first building to be built, He then moved over to the old boarding house. Mr Whiteoak certainty knows about pistols and rifles and how to fix them, this must be a skill that he picked up during the war years.

Ms Marie Williams a horse trader and horse breeder resident of Whiteoak's, she had been brought up on a ranch in Missouri until the family moved to Virginia City, Montana, in 1863, perhaps to find their fortune in the gold fields, Her brother and sister went their septate ways and had not seen each other until August last, when the Gazette wrote a small article on them meeting back up Mr P Ruston and her Sister Ms Linda Betts had come to see Ms Rayne performance at Whiteoak's. Marie is known as our very own frontierswoman and has travelled to many places and across the great plains and renowned for her horsemanship, and her cross-dressing ways (her habit of wearing men's attire) but also for her kindness towards others. Amongst her achievements she has rode with a U.S. Army troop. Also, she takes credit for rescuing a runaway stagecoach fleeing from a Cheyenne war party by bravely driving the coach and saving six passengers and a wounded driver. I once recall a place called Powder River while I was in the Army where one horse broke loose and broke the handler's arm, she singlehanded calmed the horse and brought it back to the owner, this was for a wagon train that was headed north. Whiteoak's as being a frontier town keeps no secrets, as a Horse trader, many fine horses can be bought and sold through her stables in which she manages and can be found at the back of Whiteoak's Livery or at Stenson Ranch.

No 12 Main Street Undertaker Mr Nick Garvy (Undertaker Dodger)

Mr Dodger

Meet Mr. Dodger, the friendly undertaker. He is the town's go-to mortician, he is no stranger to sombre affairs and suit-clad visitors. But what sets Mr. Dodger apart is his unique knack for lending a hand in unexpected places. When the sun sets, something magical happens - he effortlessly transforms into the life of the party, lending a helping hand behind the bar of the local saloon. With a friendly smile always etched on his face, Dodger navigates effortlessly between pouring drinks and cracking jokes, creating an atmosphere that is filled with laughter and warmth. His calm and reassuring presence has a way of making everyone feel at ease, turning strangers into friends in an instant. Dodger's ability to seamlessly transition from one role to another is a testament to his extraordinary personality and versatility. Whether he's consoling grieving families or lightening the mood with his undeniable charm, Mr. Dodger is the definition of a true gem in any community.

Mr Dodger came over from England on a steamer trying to find his fortune like many thousands he headed off to California for the Gold Rush but was widely panned out by the time he arrived, Not much else is known about Mr Dodger a very tall man and not seen much throughout the town except when there are corpses, He is married to Tasha with a son Michael, he moved to Whiteoak's as his home perished towards the end of war, he moved from town to town helping on the battlefields burying the dead for both sides, Congress authorized a national cemetery system to be operated by the Quartermaster General. This act is considered the beginning of the quartermaster mortuary affairs mission. Unfortunately, the act merely authorized the cemeteries. The Army lacked the organization, doctrine, and procedures to identify human remains and provide timely burials. But attitudes where shifting toward providing better care for the war dead. These men had given their lives for the nation, and both Soldiers and civilians believed they deserved a decent burial. Mr Dodger also helped clearing waste from towns just to make a cent or two, finally after a year or so moving from town-to-town, Mr Dodger arrived at Whiteoak's and decided to set up a small funeral parlour, By this time he was very experienced in his field had no trouble to establish himself, When trade is quiet you might find Mr Dodger in the Painted Pony Saloon working as barkeep or sometimes known as the 'Mixologist'. He also keeps an eye out for any trouble were the 'soiled doves' or 'sporting women.' while they work the Saloon.

No 13 Main Street U.S Marshal Office / Gazette Office Mr Andy Chapman (Chapper's US Marshal & Editor) Mrs Debra Chapman (Ms Debs Marshal's wife)

Meet Marshal Chapman and his lovely wife, Mrs. Debra Chapman! These two individuals are the epitome of warmth, charm, and all things friendly.

Marshal Chapman

Debra

Marshal, with his infectious smile and outgoing personality, instantly puts everyone at ease. He effortlessly connects with people from all walks of life, making each interaction feel like a genuine conversation with an old friend. As for Mrs. Chapman, her grace and quick wit are truly unmatched. Whether it's lending a helping hand or offering a listening ear, she always goes above and beyond to make others feel valued and loved. Together, Marshal and Mrs. Chapman radiate positivity and embody the true meaning of friendship. Meeting them is like discovering a ray of sunshine on a cloudy day – a joyful experience that leaves a lasting impact. So, get ready to be captivated by their warmth, as they welcome you into their world with open arms.

Marshal Andrew Chapman was born from English ancestry and growing up in the North, Known as 'Chappers', Eldest of three brothers he joined the Cavalry at a young age moving across the country mainly on patrol against hostiles and protecting supply wagons. He met Debra whilst out on patrol when they stumbled upon a homestead under attack. Debra a farm girl from Virginia and worked the on the homestead, she was youngest of 8 siblings, but unfortunately most had perished during the attack. They married not long after their first encounter and had two children, His daughter married a wealthy businessman from Washington and his son opened a grocery store in Baltimore. Chappers was also known as a fighter and often took bareknuckle boxing fights to make a few dollars when times were hard this earnt him a reputation, but deep down was a gentle family man. As war broke out Chappers re-enlisted back into the Cavalry and saw many campaigns and rose to first sergeant. After the war times were difficult, they moved around while Chappers worked for the Northern Pacific then the Great Northern protecting the railroad workers from Hostiles & Outlaws. After a tough winter they moved south and settled in Whiteoak's were Chappers took the vacant position as Marshal, and he is now responsible for the Stenson Territory and beyond. Chappers has also a part time job as the editor of the Gazette when not out catching bandits and other federal business this also keeps him busy.

No 1 2nd Street Governors Building Mr Tom Atwal (Tom Governor)

I am pleased to introduce Mr. Thomas Atwal, the esteemed Governor of Stenson County. With his extensive professional background and exceptional leadership skills, Mr. Atwal has been an instrumental figure in the development and progress of the county. As Governor, he has implemented innovative strategies to address the challenges faced by the community, working tirelessly to ensure the prosperity of its residents. Mr. Atwal's dedication to public service is reflected in his unwavering commitment to improving the quality of life for all Stenson County residents.

Mr T Atwal

Mr Thomas Atwal is a man of eastern origin whose family arrived in the US with the English before the war of Independence, His family prospered and he had good schooling and went off to study law, after Law school he joined the Republican Party, Undecided on a profession, he lobbied for better roads and transport development within the infrastructure of small towns. This soon saw Mr Atwal being voted in as Governor of Stenson a small county within the State of Texas, Times were difficult as the war had taken its toll within small area's and there was still pockets of resistance against the federal government, In small settlements like Whiteoak springs he found the benefits and opportunities for business to grow and prosper, He found people considering him to be a suitable candidate for presidency, but he declined and settled to continue as governor. Mr Atwal helped President Grant on a number of reform issues, including presidents' administration that prosecuted Mormon polygamists in 71 and vice crimes like pornography and abortion in 73. The Panic of 73 plunged the nation into a severe economic depression and financial crisis this is still happening, but the Republicans still have backing of Mr Atwal. Mr Atwal now resides on 2nd Street of Whiteoak Springs a Grand building at the end of the street and still is the Governor of Stenson.

No 1, 2nd Street Governors Building Mr John Pick (JP Barman/Hired Hand Also gunman English Jack)

John, a man of English descent, can easily be described as an educated individual - a true embodiment of an English gentleman. With a deep understanding of his profession as a barman, John effortlessly exudes professionalism in every aspect of his work. His refined mannerisms and polished communication skills make him stand out amongst the crowd, setting him apart as an exemplary barman. Whether it's his knack for recommending the perfect drink or his attention to detail in crafting each drink, John's dedication to his craft is evident in every pour. From the moment patrons walk through the doors, his warm and welcoming demeanour instantly puts them at ease, creating an inviting atmosphere that keeps them coming back for more. With his profound knowledge of spirits and an unwavering commitment to delivering impeccable service, John truly epitomizes the essence of an English gentleman in the realm of bartending.

He often travels finding adventure throughout the west. Currently he is residing at the Governors building renting a room. John often travels through serval towns such as Whiteoak's and Laredo occasionally working as a hired hand or barman to keep him occupied. He studied Law and was a Judge for a while at Mayell Creek and Spearfish Creek, There's a mystery on why he didn't continue with this profession, but some say that he saw corruption in parts of the legal system especially between local sheriffs and Town Judges, It's believed that he walked away. I do recall meeting him before Whiteoak's as I was in the Army, and he was with Ms Marie at Powder River. Also, a fine horseman he often helps at the stables and has a wide knowledge horses and ponies. You would be able to find him either at the Painted Pony Saloon or in the Governors building.

No 2, 2nd Street Triple R Cattle Company Mr Jim Ralph (J London Ranch Owner) Mr Bob Ralph (B Lonesome Ranch Owner) Mr Steve Ralph (Ranch Owner/ Mexican Bandit Antiono) Mrs Sally Ralph (Ranch Owner Wife)

The Origin of The Triple "R" Cattle Company

After the war, between the states in which both Lonesome Bob and Jim London, two Kansas volunteers from Leavenworth had fought valiantly for the Union cause. Both having been wounded and having saved the others life several times, they had, as often happens in war, became inseparable and at the end of hostilities had returned together to their hometown, There Lonesome Bob's eleven year old brother Ralph still resided with his aunt Amy, his father having been killed in a mining accident some years earlier and he himself having been too young to have taken an active part in the war. Times were hard for both sides after the war and work was hard to come by, but Jim, Bob and Ralph soon found employment at a small, struggling cattle ranch some distance from their home.

This ranch was owned by an often-sickly old timer by the name of Raymond "R" Riddick, who had called his small homestead 'The Triple "R" Cattle Company, a rather grandiose name, for such a small, dilapidated spread of land. Mr Riddick's own two sons, Raymond Junior and Ronald had both been killed in the war, and because of this The Triple "R" Cattle company was near ruin, but with the help of his three new employees the ranch began to prosper and was soon regarded with much respect amongst other ranches in the area. However, after a few years, the old timer's health began to deteriorate greatly, until finally, close to the end of his life, he called Bob, Jim and Ralph to his bedside.

"I want you to know how grateful I am to the three of you", he said, "And over the past few years have come to look on you as family. Now as you must know by now, my life is pretty much at an end, so I would take it mighty kindly if you three boys would take over the ranch as you're own". He took a deep, painful breath and continued, pushing the deeds to the ranch into Bob's hand. "If my own boys had survived, I would have given it to them, but God had other plans, and I've got no-one else. My only condition, if you would be so kind is that when I'm gone, you bury me under the big oak tree in the lower field, next to my beloved wife Etta. Go on now", he said, "you get outta' here, cause you got work to do, and I got somewhere else to be". That was the last time the three young men saw the old timer alive. And true to his wishes, they buried him under the old oak tree, next to his darling wife. Over the next few years, they worked harder than ever, and the business soon outgrew the land they had to graze their herds on.

So, reluctantly they sold the ranch, but not the business name, and bought a much larger spread of land close to the town of Whiteoak Springs in Stenson County Texas. Here the three of them built a large, luxurious log cabin, which they shared. By now they could easily have afforded to have one built for them, but they wanted to build it themselves, and as a mark of respect for the old timer that had given them their chance of a good life.

Over the front door they placed a large wooden plaque, adorned with the horns of a large longhorn steer and a brass plaque proudly proclaiming the name, The Triple "R" Cattle Company.

Some years later, young Ralph, having grown to adulthood, met and fell in love with a beautiful young woman, by the name of Miss Sally Karr. Little is known of Miss Karr's background, other than she was of English descent, and quite obviously from a well-to-do family. It was also noted among cattle barons and others that Miss Karr had a very good knowledge of the cattle industry and could easily keep up with the men in conversations on the subject, sparking rumours that she may well be related to the very well-known and influential, Sir Henry Seton-Karr, and the English aristocracy, though she would never be cornered into confirming or denying whether such rumours were true or not.

It wasn't too long after their meeting that Ralph proposed to Sally and was accepted, on the condition that they would build a home of their own and Sally would not have to share her home with three men, as this would not be considered proper.

So, with this agreed, and after a two-year engagement, in which time they torn down the old bunkhouse and built their own marital cabin they were wed.

No 3 2nd Street Vacant The Old Doc's Building, formally Mick and Alex. known as E Blackwell Doctor & Surgeon (The couple have now left the town community) But now David Archer and Linda Betts (Mose & Lil) have recently taken over the premises.

The building will be turned into the 'Lils house of ill repute' and Mose a Deputy Marshal.

No 4 2nd Street Court House & Pinkerton Agency Mr Adam Riddleston ('Lawdog' Pinkerton) Mrs Kerry Riddleston (Judge Pee) Ned & Layla Riddleston The Shoeshine Shack The Fields (Blue Eyes and Creature Moonshine)

Meet Judge Pee and "Lawdog" the Pinkerton, a dynamic duo of justice, always ready to protect the innocent and uphold the law with unwavering determination. Their unique partnership was bolstered by the presence of two courageous children, Blue Eyes and Creature Moonshine, whose bright spirits illuminated even the darkest corners. With their boundless curiosity and hearty laughter, Blue Eyes and Creature Moonshine added a touch of wonder to every escapade.

'Lawdog' is an only child son of a peeler and grandson of a rural constable. He has tried Effortlessly to become a policeman but rejected due to height requirements. Feeling shamed in not being able to follow in his families' footsteps he boarded a steamer to New York to seek a law enforcement career in this fast wild country. Following a drunken brawl over a card game with the first mate on the steamer, he was then held in quarantine in New York, until the authorities could decide how he could pay of the debt. 'Lawdog' suggested that he could Join the New York Police but with the strong Irish constituent objected as he was English after several week in custody in the Quarantine pen he was approached by the Pinkerton Detective Agency looking for young, educated men for duties such as hired guards in coal, iron, and lumber disputes in Illinois, Michigan, New York, Pennsylvania, and West Virginia. The Pinkerton Detective

Agency is believed to be the largest private law enforcement organization in the world. Lawdog was moved to Whiteoak Springs to Protect the Thomas Trust and Savings Bank and the silver mine a long with Mr Thomas they serve the area, Not long after arriving in Whiteoak's Lawdog met Judge Pee.

Miss Pee, an orphaned child from Indiana who was sponsored by Arabella Mansfield (the first female admitted to the US Bar), dedicated herself to learning law and worked tirelessly to raise herself from her lowly beginnings. After passing her bar with high scores bearing in mind that the law the bar exam was restricted to "males over 21," like Arabella she excelled in the subject and as a reward Miss Pee was sent to Whiteoak Springs as her first placement to prove herself as Judge Pee. This has proven to be wise choice as Whiteoak's being frontier town many cases have and will go through her Court house making her name throughout Stenson County Many have said that she is a tough as the outlaws that are on trial.

Blue Eyes and Creature - Moonshine Shoeshine Shack are Brother and Sister who ran away from home because of a cruel stepmother who their father had recently taken as his wife. Determined to avoid any further beatings, they headed off young, vulnerable, and alone. After encountering many toils and turmoil along the route, they finally found themselves at Whiteoak Springs and were given the chance by the Governor there to renovate a small shack to call their home and have started to develop a business of shoe-shining to fund their existence in the town.

No 5 2nd Street Saddlery Mr Monty Tubb (Mony Saddler) Mrs Tubb (Mags/Maggie)

Monty **Maggie**

Monty the saddler and his wife Maggie are truly the epitome of a delightful couple, radiating warmth and genuine kindness. Monty, with his skilled craftsmanship and unwavering passion for leatherwork, brings life to every piece he touches. Every stitch is carefully crafted, reflecting his dedication and love for his craft. Meanwhile, Maggie exudes an enchanting charm, always greeting customers with a smile that can light up a room. Her inviting demeanour and genuine interest in people make each visit to their quaint shop an unforgettable experience. Together, Monty and Maggie create an atmosphere that is both welcoming and comforting; a place where individuals can share their stories and aspirations while indulging in the beauty of handmade leather goods.

I Monty was born in the state of Virginia into a very large family, My father was always off traveling trying to raise money to support his family so it was left us boys to provide food and tend the farm and by the age of around ten years of age I had become a very good marksman with a musket and tracker, Around the age of thirteen or fourteen I was sold into an apprenticeship with the local leather merchant which was to last seven years, it was while working in the shop the first of what would be many encounters that would shape my life occurred, A man who I later discovered was Jedediah Smith arrived needing his horse harness repaired while I was repairing the tackle he mentioned he was on his way to Saint Louis to join a group of one hundred single fit young men to trap beaver in the wind river area of Wyoming for a year, After he had left I could not put the idea of trapping and exploring the vast continent of America out of my mind I must have had my father's wandering feet, so a couple of days later I took my musket and possibles bag and headed for St Louis, I arrived too late, and the army of trappers had already left for the wind river. I found the man who had hired the men and asked for a job which I was turned down because of my age only being about seventeen. Knowing I couldn't go home because I had broken my terms of apprenticeship and would be arrested I tried to find employment in St Louis but with no joy I was about to give up and go home to whatever awaited me when the second encounter occurred I met a couple of freelance trappers who invited me to join them so with what little money I had left I bought traps powder and some other necessities and l left for the wind river to make my fortune,

After many years of trapping beaver and buffalo and learning the lay of the land and fighting with the natives the trapping of beaver stopped (seams the British had grown bored with beaver hats and turned to silk). I found myself in independence Missouri being hired as a scout for the wagon trains heading to the promised lands of Oregon and it was on one of those journeys I saw the most beautiful girl I'd ever seen, By the time we reached Oregon we had fallen in love and got married and decided to settle down, I knew great piece of land on the fork of the Oregon trail and we built a trading post to supply the constant flow of wagons heading to Oregon and now California Maggie tending the store and I repairing harness and other leather goods but as before with the beaver the traveller slowed and trade dried up we sold the trading post to the government for an army fort and headed for California and the gold fields,

We arrived in the gold fields just as the gold was petering out scratching around for a while with very poor return, We met a man who was going to Texas saying it was a vast state with plenty of opportunities so off to Texas we went traveling around trying to scratch a living when we came upon the town of Whiteoak's springs the towns folk were very friendly and welcoming and seeing they had no Saddler we decided with their blessing to settle down there and open a shop making and repairing saddles and other leather goods.

No 6 2nd Street Blacksmith Mr Pete West (Big Sam, Blacksmith/Bandit) Ms Jackie Waller (Crystaljak, Sharpshooter, Blacksmiths Wife)

Big Sam **Crystaljak**

Welcome to Big Sam and Crystaljak, the charming blacksmith and his delightful wife situated in the heart of Whiteoak's. Prepare to be captivated by the warmth and friendliness that emanates from this lovely couple. As you step into their humble abode, you'll be greeted with a genuine smile and a firm handshake, instantly making you feel like part of their extended family. Big Sam's sturdy hands and skilful craftsmanship meld the raw elements into beautiful creations.

Big Sam worked on the cattle drives for many years, he was born in Wyoming on a small homestead he was left an orphan at a young age having to fend for himself. Within a short span of time, he found himself at the helm of a small but promising posse of vibrant young cowboys, entrusted with the momentous task of driving cattle from the vast plains of Wyoming all the way down to the vibrant landscapes of Mexico. He enjoyed his life although it was tough, and he had few possessions of his own. During his time in Mexico, Big Sam encountered an unexpected twist of fate when he found himself entangled with a notorious group of Mexican bandits. Known for their cattle rustling and horse theft activities along the border, these bandits were not to be trifled with. In a peculiar case of mistaken identity, Big Sam found himself at the centre of their attention. Realizing the danger of being associated with such criminals, he made the difficult decision to abandon the cattle drive, he was left to forge a new path in life, And he hastily fled Mexico with the knowledge that the bandits would stop at nothing to silence him. Little did he know that this abrupt escape would lead him down an unexpected journey.

He travelled the along arduous journey North, to Montanna where he found a small ranch, Helping to break in horses and to help the local blacksmith who taught him the art of smithing, he provided shoes for the horses on the ranch. As the war broke out, the Army brought most of the horses from the ranch, Big Sam continued to work at the Ranch, but work was scarce, then a tragic turn of events occurred, the owner of the ranch died suddenly, and his family couldn't agree who would run the ranch - following a gun battle between the children, Big Sam decided that ranch life was too dangerous and left for the open plains. By this time, the war was already well into its later years, and with a desire to stay out of harm's way, he decided to join the Army as a farrier. He figured that working with horses and maintaining their hooves would be a safer option compared to being on the treacherous front lines.

A quiet man, who normally turned away from conflict, He found himself between a rock and a hard place and he decided to desert. Living as a drifter, constantly glancing over his shoulder, fearing the Army might catch up with him. As he made his way through the treacherous great plains, dangers lurked at every turn, not just from hostiles but also from cavalry patrols. However, fate had a kind twist waiting for him in Nebraska. It was there that he stumbled upon a trading post, and to his surprise, he learned that the war had ended.

Not far from the trading post, there existed a small settlement where various tribes coexisted alongside mixed-race children. In this harmonious blend of cultures, a widower named Crystaljak stood out as a respected figure with a large collection of stones, With her stones, she dedicated herself to the noble cause of healing. The Indians, recognizing the parallels between her practices and those of their own medicine men, graciously granted her unrestricted passage across the vast plains. During her travels, she ventured far and wide, visiting mountain men, as well as individuals from different walks of life, irrespective of their ethnicity. Her mission was clear - to share the power of her healing stones with everyone she encountered and to engage in trade with the Indians. Through her actions, she bridged cultural divides and fostered understanding.

Crystaljak's journey took an unexpected turn when a seasoned mountain man took her under his wing and taught her the art of shooting. With unwavering determination, she swiftly honed her skills and transformed into a proficient sharpshooter, never missing her mark. Her exceptional marksmanship was more than just a matter of self-defence against the perils of predators that lurked during her travels; it also served as a shield against cunning outlaws and opportunistic vagabonds who coveted her valuable trading goods. While at the trading post she met Big Sam, Crystaljak decided to spent some time with Big Sam travelling together, after a couple of years wondering through the wilds, They realized a mutual longing for a place to call home, leading them to establish themselves in a frontier town known as Whiteoak's, where they built a barn and cabin, Big Sam, a skilled blacksmith, once again dedicated his time and expertise to crafting shoes for horses in his well-equipped forge. Not only did Big Sam demonstrate his craftsmanship in horseshoe making, but he also catered to the needs of the local community by fashioning various metal tools. Crystaljak cherished her precious healing stones, holding onto them tightly as a comforting reminder of her inner strength and her past healing. However, what brought them both even greater solace was the newfound serenity at Whiteoak's where nobody pried into their past.

No 7 2nd Street Old No 7 Mining co Mr Chris Dennett (Cole Rayburn Mine Owner) Mr John Dennett (JD Rayburn Mine Owner)

Cole Rayburn

JD Rayburn

Cole Rayburn, a passionate mine owner, and his brother JD Rayburn. These two adventurous brothers embarked on an unforgettable journey in the small town of Whiteoak's, where they stumbled upon a remarkable discovery - silver! With their unwavering determination and a pinch of luck, they unearthed a vast silver deposit that left everyone in awe. Their efforts not only transformed their own lives but also had a tremendous impact on the community. With a friendly tone, it's truly inspiring to see the power of exploration and the triumph of two brothers who turned a small town into a mining hub, all while nurturing a sense of camaraderie among the locals. The story of Cole and JD Rayburn is a testament to the indomitable spirit of adventure and the wonders that can be found when we dare to explore.

Cole and JD Rayburn from Alum Creek West Virginia Cole youngest son & JD second oldest of three Brothers, Mitch is the eldest he left when he was 18 believed to be in Montana. Cole & JD set off for the California gold rush, which was well established at the point, once the brothers were in California they fell upon hard times and were unable to find gold as most sites had been panned out. Diane, wife of Cole started to sell pies to keep the pair afloat and avoiding the war

the pair travelled through the states trying their luck at different enterprises from town-to-town. One day on their travels Cole noticed that Whiteoak's had the right geographical location for silver the pair invested all they had to stake a mine, They finally struck silver and being successful the brothers now manage the Mine. The mine is now in its second phase now and is looking for workers to recruit, Mr C Rayburn said you must find your own accommodation while working at the mine and its long hours, but you are rewarded well, Whiteoak's has attracted many passers-by so there's no shortage of workers. You can find the pair in the Mining office, if not they would be in the Saloon.

No 8 2nd Street Chapel Mr Mark Winnett (Preacher) Mrs Tanya Winnett (Preachers' wife)

Meet Mark the Preacher and his wife, Tan! These two are an incredibly warm and welcoming couple, always spreading love and positivity wherever they go. Mark, with his vibrant personality and infectious smile, embodies the true spirit of a preacher. His sermons are not only uplifting, but also thought-provoking, leaving you with a sense of inner peace and motivation. And then there's Tan, his supportive and delightful wife. Tan's gentle nature and kind heart make her the perfect companion for Mark. Together, they make it a point to make everyone feel like part of their extended family, creating an inclusive and hospitable environment for everyone they encounter. Whether you're seeking spiritual guidance or simply a friendly conversation, Mark the Preacher and Tan are the couple to turn to. With their friendly demeanour and genuine love for others, they are sure to leave a lasting impression on your heart.

Preacher known to everyone, settled in Whiteoak's in 73 and started to build a small church for the town Christian followers. Preacher

and his wife travelled throughout Preaching the Gospel, The war was America's bloodiest conflict. The unprecedented violence of battles such as Shiloh, Antietam, Stones River, and Gettysburg shocked citizens and international observers alike and people needed condolence Preachers such as Mark and his wife were vital for people looking for some divine truths & answers, And the pair travelled teaching the gospel throughout the southern states. His wife Tan travelled everywhere with him also preaching the word of God. With constant threat from Comanches he was advised to purchase a pistol and a Bowie knife before taking his new post in Indian country. Presiding elder Ivey H. Cox told Preacher he needed a pony, saddlebags, lariat, Bible, and hymnal. Firmly believing in the teaching that the Lord helped those who helped themselves. Preacher and Tan soon became weary of travelling and lucky to have their scalps upon their heads, they found a small frontier town without the Christian ways and soon started preaching in the beginning everybody came armed and the corners of a small house were stacked with rifles and shotguns, but it soon became a regular congregation and they decided to build a small church.

No 9 Belle End. The Haberdashery Mrs Margaret Dunkley (Mags's haberdasher) Mr Arthur Dunkley (Trailer' retired cowhand)

Trailer **Mags**

Trailer, the retired cowhand, and Mags, the talented haberdasher, make quite the dynamic duo in their small western town. With their unique set of skills and friendly personalities, these two have become beloved figures in the community. Trailer, a weathered cowboy with years of experience under his belt, has an infectious laugh and a knack for spinning tall tales around the campfire. Meanwhile, Mags, the master of all things hats and accessories, brings a touch of style and flair to every outfit in the town.

Mighty and Trailer and their faithful dog Sadie they travelled around many small towns throughout the West trailer finding work as a ranch hand on small ranches, Small ranches often value individuals who possess a strong work ethic, reliability, and a genuine interest in the day-to-day operations. Additionally, having a diverse set of skills such as animal husbandry is essential and in local ranching community can also prove beneficial, as word-of-mouth referrals are common in this tight-knit industry, As they travelled through state to state Maggie using her skills as a Seamstress, mending worn out clothes and making new, They finally settled in a settlement of Deadwood, Deadwood began illegally in the 1870s, on land which had been granted to the Lakota people in the 1868 Treaty of Fort Laramie. The treaty had guaranteed ownership of the Black Hills to the Lakota people, who consider this area to be sacred. The settlers' squatting led to numerous land disputes, several of which reached the United States Supreme Court. Custer led an expedition into the Black Hills and announced the discovery of gold in 1874, on French

Creek near present-day Custer, South Dakota. This announcement was a catalyst for the Black Hills Gold Rush, and miners and entrepreneurs swept into the area. There Trailer and Maggie found it easy to acquire enough work. But word had travelled that another Frontier Town had recently sprung up, but south in Texas, Black hills were winters was harsh so Maggie and Trailer with Sadie decided to travel the treacherous Journey South to Whiteoak's Springs, They faced many Perils including hostile encounters with restless natives, The weather also had taken its toll on the pair, and as they reached Whiteoak's, the pair received an overwhelming welcome and decided to stay, With the help from towns community spirit, they were able set up a small cabin and Workshop were Maggie continues to provide her seam stressing skills and has opened up a Haberdashery while Trailer took the odd job helping out with the Triple R Cattle company. You can find then at Belle End next to the Church.

No 1 Lincoln Corner Wells Fargo & Co, Pony Express Mrs Andrea Frost (Post Mistress) Mr Martin Frost ('Wonbag' Coach Master & Groom, Pony express)

Here at Wells Fargo & Co, we are proud to introduce two integral members of our team: Mrs. Andrea, the dedicated Post Mistress, and Martin, the 'Wonbag' Coach Master of our esteemed Pony Express branch. With their unwavering commitment and expertise, they ensure that our customers' mail is delivered promptly and efficiently. Mrs. Andrea exemplifies true friendliness, always greeting customers with a warm smile and offering assistance with any postal needs. Martin, on the other hand, channels his passion for ponies and coaching into overseeing the smooth operation of our Pony Express services. Together, they form an incredible team, providing friendly and reliable postal services to our valued customers. At Wells Fargo & Co, we take great pride in the exceptional individuals like Mrs. Andrea and Martin who contribute to our commitment to excellence.

Andrea, a former Postmistress from a small village in Staffordshire met Martin, a groom for the local Manor House, Andrea very much in control of the complex and demanding tasks of a rapidly growing Post Offices which required a salaried female official in charge of PO operations and staff within a specific area defined by its Postal Village. Duties and responsibilities were the same as those of Postmasters, but fewer career opportunities for women, meant that Postmistresses were generally in charge of smaller locations and had accordingly lower average salaries than their Postmaster colleagues. But soon romance bloomed as a young man Martin, caught her eye and the pair soon married, but Andrea's role in the Post office was in jeopardy, as her father disapproved of their marriage as former Clergyman and had a lot of influence throughout the village, So the pair gathered enough money to catch a steamship to New York to escape leaving everything behind. After difficulties to secure a job Andrea managed to find employment at Wells Fargo Co and was posted to San Francisco at Wells Fargo Express, Montgomery St. As a general clerk, For Martin it was easy he managed to get employment at a local livery. The pair enjoyed their roles but started to be adventurous and wanted to see more of the frontier and its dangers. Although skilled roles were difficult to find after talking to a Fargo agent, Andrea managed to secure a post to Wells Fargo Co and Express in Whiteoak Springs. This was the ideal posting, the pair were looking for a frontier town and a sense of adventure, Andrea with her postal experience would oversee the Stagecoach, Passengers and letters, while Martin would be responsible for looking after the horses, so he could change the horses from a long journey or to feed and water them on short journeys. In 74, Martin and Andrea packed their bags and set off for Whiteoak's from San Francisco as before they knew it would be a long journey but by this time travel was made easier by Railroad. They made it safely and reside at No 1 Lincoln Corner Wells Fargo & Co, Pony Express.

N o 1 The Fields Texas Rangers Office Mr Steve Forber (Poncho, Ranger) Mr Dave Kirkman (Soapy, Ranger)

Meet Texas Ranger Soapy, a true embodiment of the Wild West spirit with a dash of charm. From his rugged cowboy hat to his dusty boots, Soapy exudes an undeniable sense of adventure and camaraderie. With a warm smile and a firm handshake, he welcomes all who cross his path with open arms. A veteran of the Texas Rangers, Soapy's jovial nature belies his fearless dedication to upholding justice and protecting the innocent. Whether he's tracking down outlaws or lending a helping hand in his community. You can often find him regaling folks with his captivating tales by the campfire, effortlessly captivating both young and old with his larger-than-life adventures. Soapy's friendly demeanour and approachable personality make him a beloved figure in the hearts of those lucky enough to call him a friend. So, next time you find yourself in the Lone Star State, keep an eye out for the legend that is Texas Ranger Soapy.

9th January 1845: David Kirkman the son of Robert Lomax Kirkman and Mary Lawson of Breightmet Fold, Breightmet, Bolton, Lancashire, England, was born. On the 25th of May 1856, My family and myself along with other members of the Saints departed from Liverpool, Lancashire aboard the ship 'Horizon' as part of the Latter-Day Saints (Mormons) migration to Zion, Salt Lake, Salt Lake City,

Utah, America. 30th June 1856: We arrived in Boston, Massachusetts, and from there we all travelled by train to Iowa City, Iowa, where we joined the Edward Martin Handcart company.

25th August 1856: We left Iowa City even though father had been offered work and had decided to accept the offer, (This was because the other saints wanted him to travel with them) The 576 who left Iowa were to travel 1,300 miles overland pulling our belongings on handcarts that we had made in Iowa. We had to stop unexpectedly in Florence, Nebraska to repair some of the badly made handcarts, and it is because of this we left Iowa late in the year and got caught in the winter blizzards and freezing weather and had to take shelter.

11th November 1856: Father passed away along with my baby brother, Peter due to lack of food and the freezing cold, we thawed the ground as much as we could so we could bury father and our Peter, They now lie in Martins Cove, Sweetwater, Wyoming.

30th November 1856: With the help of rescue parties sent by Brigham Young from Salt Lake City we finally reached our destination with the loss of 145 people. That is when things started to go wrong for me as I was looking for someone to blame for fathers' death. Only for the other saints we would have stayed in Iowa for the winter, and we would have still been a complete family. To make matters worse mother remarried hastily.

23rd March 1857: Mother married a man senior to herself, He was 70 years of age and very respected within the Latter-Day Saints. Having a rebellious stepson did not go down to well with him and I found myself being treated differently to the other children in the household. That is when I decided the Church of the Latter-Day Saints was not for me. For the next few years, I spent all of my time with the Vaqueros (Cowboys) learning about cattle drives, guns and how to shoot and horses as I had already decided this was to be my life. 9th January 1860: On the night of my 15th birthday when everyone in the house were sleeping, I saddled a horse and stole what little money I could find. I Gathered my belongings and rode out leaving my mother, brothers and The Latter-Day Saints behind me to start a new life.

As a drifter you come across and see things that can help you survive these lands, So on my way to Texas I drifted in and out of towns usually leaving my mark behind me as I would help myself to whatever I needed or wanted either by fair means or foul!

During the Civil War that raged across the country from 1861-1865 I showed no loyalty to either side only to myself and my survival and was known to kill men on both sides that was until I joined up with Col John S Mosby and his Raiders of the Confederate States Army, We were better known as guerrilla fighters and our job was to disrupt Union forces in hit and run raids which we did with great success. (At the end of the war we never surrendered we just went our separate ways with our ill-gotten gains) After the war, I finally made my way to Texas to work as a Cattle Drover and that is where I met Major John B Jones of the Texas Rangers frontier battalion, I was recruited as a Ranger to Protect the homesteaders from bandits that came across the border, That is where I met Poncho and where (Utah changed into Soapy) In 1876 Poncho and myself were posted to a small frontier town called Whiteoak Springs, To assist the Town Marshall and Town sheriff to keep peace and to protect the town.

Meet Texas Ranger Poncho, a seasoned lawman with a spirit as bold as the wild west itself. With his trusty steed by his side and a steely gaze that never wavers, Poncho fearlessly ventures into the unknown, chasing down outlaws and upholding justice. From dusty saloons to treacherous desert trails, he fearlessly embarks on daring adventures, fuelled by his unwavering commitment to protect the innocent. With each mission, Poncho's courage shines through, as he faces danger head-on and never backs down from a fight. Whether he's tracking fugitives through rugged canyons or unravelling complex mysteries, this intrepid lawman is a force to be reckoned with. So, hold on tight and prepare to join Texas Ranger Poncho.

Poncho was born in Iowa a long time ago now. My God given name has long since been forgotten 'cept by me, of course. My ma and pa were good folk and bore not only me but five others too. Three boy, three girls. I was the last born. I went south and west as soon as I was able mainly to relieve the burden on my parents. It wasn't easy for them to raise such a pestle O'Berns. I took to the mountain and had many adventures, and it was there that I got my now known as name. Poncho. T'was from an old timer and mentor Caleb Jones. He saw me wearing an old poncho I'd picked up some place, and he just came right out with the name, and it stuck! It was by the banks of the Greasy Grass river at rendezvous, I met up with my pard Soapy. We too to trapping together and found ourselves moving further and further south until we ended up in Texas. Beaver was playing out, so we joined the Rangers. Then came the War Of Northern Aggression. So, we joined the grey and headed east to fight. Soapy, being of independent mind and bullish will, took to doing his own thing. I kept my head down and powder dry and came out of the terrible conflict with a ball in my leg and a scar in the never-you-mind. 1865.

Defeated and beaten we returned to a very different Texas. Poverty and starvation abounded. I, along with a returned and changed Soapy, became Rangers once again. (Frontier Battalion) To complete this very short resume, we found ourselves posted to a backwater town called Whiteoak's. We made out HQ on the edge of the God forsaken hell hole in an old, deceased ex trappers' cabin who had gone by the name of Hatchet Jack. That's about it for now I guess. Not much of a tale but true, by God.

Chapter 3

In the Beginning:

As day breaks, an air of adventure permeates the landscape as the sun rises above the majestic hills. It casts a golden hue on the landscape, where the Civil War is nearing its climactic end. The echoes of cannon fire still reverberate in the ear of many, but there is an evident shift in the winds. The tides of destiny have turned, and the balance of power has tilted towards the North. Many Southern troops, once valiant and fierce, have been routed or have chosen to surrender. Amidst the remnants of broken alliances and shattered dreams, a glimmer of hope emerges, igniting the spirits of those who remain.

A small band of partisan raiders was involved in many fights, raiding supply lines and observation posts throughout Missouri, with the fear of being captured, the band of men moved towards Texas to winter, These numerous renegades and Confederate troops played a significant role in the conflict. These renegades, often referred to as guerillas or bushwhackers, operated outside the traditional military structures and caused havoc behind Union lines. Many didn't surrender and headed south to Texas, New Mexico, or Mexico in fear of being killed or hunted down. One particular raider Mr A Whiteoak moved south with a small band of men, it's not clear who they rode for, but later some people believed it was bloody Bill Anderson. After riding a long journey along the Texas panhandle and heading towards the Mexican border. The trail south to the border was the same for men and beasts, and it led through hell. They embarked on a thrilling journey, navigating through treacherous terrains and untamed wilderness. After endless days of exploration, they stumbled upon a hidden sanctuary, a serene and secluded spot. It seemed like nature itself had conspired to create the perfect haven for them to set up camp for the winter.

The terrain was teeming with abundant resources, promising a bountiful existence amidst the harshness of the wilderness. As they ventured further, trekking an arduous 13 miles past rocky formations and the mesmerizing beauty of a ravine, A sense of awe overwhelmed their weary souls. This quiet place, tucked away from the hustle and bustle of the world, beckoned them to embrace its solitude and find solace and peace even if was only for a month or so. They could already envision the crackling campfire, the aroma of freshly brewed coffee, and the captivating starlit nights that awaited them in this idyllic corner. There before them a clearing appeared with an abandoned cabin in ruins, with a nearby spring it was perfect to winter, Tony with his small band of men they set up camp, arrival of the rains prompted him to take action and repair the cabin. With a bold determination, he embarked on a plan to ensure the cabin remained watertight, after several days chopping logs, and repairing the roof the cabin was habitable for them to shelter. After a couple of months had past, the weather was setting in and two of the men where itching to ride back to rejoin the cause. After a vote the men had decided to leave, Just leaving Tony, he knew he made the right choice to stay, as later he found out the rest of the men had found their demise, they were either hung or shot by Union Troops. Tony's supplies were getting low, he mounted up to check out the area, He knew that Fort Worth was about two week's rides, where settlers still held slaves, When the question came to secede from the Union, most citizens were for secession, and Tarrant County voted for it. The effects of the Civil War and Reconstruction nearly wiped Fort Worth off the map. At this time the forts population dropped as low as hundred and seventy-five. Food, supply, and money shortages burdened the citizens, Tony decided to ride on to try and secure supplies for him to last winter unknowing the situation at Fort Worth. As he neared the town and made his way through the dense underbrush, a sudden rustle caught his attention. He froze in his tracks, a surge of adrenaline coursing through his veins. Peeking through the foliage, his eyes widened as he came across a Union patrol with their rifles at the ready. These seasoned soldiers were on a mission, hunting down partisans and any remnants of the defeated army that still resisted surrender. But fear did not grip him. Instead, a bold determination flickered in his eyes as he contemplated his next move. The element of surprise was on his side, and he knew he had to act swiftly but there were too many for him to take on himself, possible if he had a chance he could ride away and encircle and try and pick them off, then a sudden interruption caught him off guard. A young, impeccably dressed man sauntered over, exuding confidence in every step. With a bold tone of voice, he stated, "Well, it seems you're in a little predicament." The enigmatic stranger's smirk suggested that he relished the opportunity to interject himself into Tony's chaotic moment. The interruption was unexpected, yet the stranger's confident demeanour demanded attention. Intrigue mingled with irritation as the man reluctantly acknowledged the stranger's presence, wondering what daring solution lay behind that smug face.

Let me introduce myself, I'm Mr Atwal," Tony was unsure, this man of eastern origin seemed to appear out of nowhere, Tony couldn't quite understand, a man of colour very well dressed out in the middle of the wilds, But unknown to Tony, Mr Atwal was a keen politician and owned most of the land at Stenson County from his forefathers. He was looking at the tracks, to improve the roads and transport, also development within the infrastructure of small towns and counties. With unyielding confidence, he declared to Tony, "Let me give you some assistance." Without hesitation, he strode towards the Union patrol, exuding an air of audacity, as he knew Tony was a stranger in these parts, a display of remarkable persuasive skills, he managed to convincingly to portray Tony as his trustworthy accomplice. With eloquent words and a calm demeanour, he spun a narrative that seemed flawless, leaving no room for doubt. His professionalism in handling the situation was truly commendable. As an expert in the art of manipulation the patrol rode off. Leaving Tony ensnared in a debt of gratitude, After several minutes of conversation with Mr Atwal, he then learnt that the land the abandoned cabin was on had belonged to Mr Atwal, Given the circumstances, Tony made a conscious decision to remain, his current situation he recognizes it to be a significant opening to alter his fortunes and follow a different path.

The pair soon became friends, Tony helped Mr Atwal on several occasions, and he was most appreciative of the help. After the war Mr Atwal supported President Grant in reform and the rebuild. Many Union Troops intensified the rounding up of any renegades and confederate troops that didn't surrender. On April 6, 1866, Johnson issued a second proclamation that formally ended the rebellion in Alabama, Arkansas, Florida, Georgia, Louisiana, Mississippi, North Carolina, South Carolina, and Virginia (as well as proclaiming it ended, rather than merely "suppressed," in Tennessee). Only Texas, where small pockets of resistance remained, was excluded. Tony knew he had to be careful not to be arrested or even shot, these times were dangerous. With unease Tony approached Mr Atwal and requested if he could buy the run-down cabin with the little money he had and develop it into a working ranch, as before the war he had been a farmer, but his property was burnt down by Union troops, He saw the land was good, and he had experience in running a farm as he explained to Mr Atwal, who found it difficult to refuse. Tony started to mark out the boundary and rename the Ranch to Stenson, nearby was a small Spring he named Whiteoak.

Over the course of several months, Mr. Atwal took the initiative to check in on Tony frequently, eager to see how he was progressing. It was evident that Mr. Atwal's involvement had a profound impact on Tony's life. Through his support and guidance, Mr. Atwal had managed to make a significant difference in Tony's journey. The cabin had been reshaped and fencing had been put in place and the beginnings of a barn had started to take shape. Around 13 miles north of the Whiteoak Spring there was a ravine and the rocks in the sunrise looked like fingers, a good place to hide supplies or any wondering compatriots, Tony named it Deadman's finger.

One morning Tony headed off to Fort Worth to get some supplies, by this time his face was recognised and was no longer a stranger in these parts, which made life easier while union patrols were still abundant, As Tony stepped out of the store, his eyes couldn't help but be drawn to the peculiar scene unfolding before him. Three wagons, old but sturdy, had arranged themselves neatly outside the establishment. Yet, what truly captured Tony's attention was the figure perched upon a majestic white-grey horse. It was a woman unlike any he had ever encountered, clad in buckskins, A cloud of dust surrounded her, indicating a long and arduous journey. Intrigued, Tony couldn't resist the urge to approach her with he's curious nature, With a friendly tip of his hat, he greeted the woman, "Morning Mam." Turning her gaze towards him, the woman's stern expression softened as she replied, "Git ain't nothing to see here, Mr, if you know what's good for ya." Despite her cautionary words, she reached into a pouch hanging from her buckskins and skilfully rolled a smoke. Tony moved closer with a friendly smile on his face and sincerely said, "Sorry, ma'am, if I've offended you." He wanted to ensure that his words conveyed both regret and a genuine desire just to talk with the Woman, Tony casually asked, "Where are you heading?" With a slight hint of amusement and admiration, she glanced over and retorted, "You're a persistent one, ain't ya, just like a bobcat!" With a warm smile, she explained, "We're actually headed to South Carolina. This young family is all set to start their very own lumber business, and I've been assigned to be their guide. So, if there's nothing else, Mr., I'll be on my way shortly." Tony approached the woman again and without any explanation, he politely asked, "Excuse me, may I ask your name?" However, as he awaited her response, he noticed the woman's piercing stare, one that could send shivers down the spines of most men. "Ms. Marie, now git," She replied, Despite the intensity of her gaze, Ms. Marie's response carried a hint of amusement. "Mr, you're an inquisitive one, ain't ya?" she quipped. "Just like my ex-husband, he hated my habit of wearing men's attire." Tony quickly realized he had unintentionally offended her. With a friendly tone of voice, he apologized for his intrusion, hoping to smooth over the situation. "I didn't mean to pry, Ms. Marie. I simply thought you might be interested in settling for a while at my small homestead. We could use some help with livestock, and it might provide you a peaceful sanctuary for a while" "Sorry, Mr," She replied with a friendly tone, her voice filled with regret. Tony nodded understandingly, recognizing that her decision was final. "If you ever change your mind," he said warmly, "I'll be in Stenson County, just 13 miles away from an extraordinary rock formation known as Deadman's Fingers. It's quite a sight, impossible to miss." As she gathered the reins and gave a gentle kick to her horse's flanks, the wagon train slowly began to move on. On Tonys way back to Stenson he couldn't help but reflect on his recent encounter with Ms. Marie.

Several months had flown by, and Tony had truly immersed himself in his work on the ranch. Today was no exception, as he toiled away on the barn, sweat dripping down his forehead. Lost in thought, he suddenly caught a glimpse of movement in the distance. Squinting his eyes, he could make out the figure of a rider on a magnificent white-grey horse. His heart skipped a beat as excitement flooded through him as he knew only one person that owned a white-grey horse, As the rider got closer, the figure became clearer, and indeed, it was none other than Ms. Marie. As Tony came down from the barn to welcome her, he couldn't help but become instantly captivated by the warm smile that graced her face. As he eagerly showed her around, he couldn't help but think back to the day they first met a few months ago and how coarse she was towards him, but now everything seemed different As time went on, something remarkable happened. Ms. Marie not only excelled in helping with the livestock, but she also formed an unexpected bond with Tony. Their partnership in work slowly transformed into a genuine friendship some say romance. The animals thrived under Marie's care, thanks to her tireless efforts and deep understanding of their needs. Beyond simply working together, Tony and Marie would often be found sharing stories, laughter, and moments of light-hearted banter sitting on the porch of now their homestead.

As the barn neared completion, Tony took a moment to rest in his chair, savouring a cup of coffee, while Marie was busy with the horses, However, his tranquillity was suddenly interrupted by the sight of two men approaching him. Instinctively, Tony's professional instincts kicked in, causing him to swiftly grab his trusty 12-gauge shotgun. With a measured sense of caution, he assessed the situation, ensuring he was prepared for any potential threat. The quiet stillness was replaced with an air of alertness, As the tension hung thick in the air, the two men cautiously dismounted their horses, their eyes fixed on Tony ahead. With a persuasive tone, one of them raised his voice to break the silence, expressing their peaceful intentions, "We don't want any trouble," he called out, his voice steady and unwavering. In an attempt to diffuse the escalating situation, he emphasized that they were not armed, their empty hands held out as a symbol of goodwill. Each step they took was deliberate and slow, aiming to convey their sincere desire for a peaceful resolution. In this tense moment, their persuasive words sought to create a bridge of understanding, hoping that their vulnerability and words of assurance would be enough to quell any suspicion and avoid further conflict. Tony could see that they had no holster by their side but stayed cautious, Tony said to them "What's your business in these parts", he knew that two bounty hunters had rode through only days earlier, Allow us to regale you with our thrilling tale of discovery and adventure! We are none other than Cole Rayburn and JD Rayburn, intrepid prospectors and brothers who have journeyed all the way from the sun kissed lands of California. With the wild spirit coursing through our veins, we have set out to seek our fortunes in unchartered territories. Armed with our trusty picks and spades, We have braved treacherous terrains, crossed roaring rivers, it's been a long hard journey we would like to bed down for the night, Tony agreed and lowered his 12 gauge he said there's a small outbuilding you can rest there for the evening, Tony was still very cautious of the two men.

Morning came, Tony went out to check on the men and the horses, but there was no sign of the two men, he thought this was odd? This unexpected turn of events left Tony perplexed, He went on to collect wood to light his fire, about an hour had gone by still the men hadn't returned, Tony went over to check on the horses again to see if there was any identification on who the men really were, he started to feel a little suspicious, suddenly out of the growth of the bushes the two appeared, and said to Tony, "We have seen a small piece of land yonder just past those bushes and we would like to stake a claim". "you had better make your way over and I would be able to tell you who owns the land. After a long conversation Tony agreed for the two men to meet Mr Atwal. A few days later Mr Atwal sold them a small stake in the land so the brothers could mine, Mr Atwal was quite shrewd when it came to business and would take a cut of profits if anything was found, Tony was awarded a small fee for introducing the men to him.

JD Rayburn and Cole boldly staked their claim for the piece of land, the mine that had captivated their adventurous souls. With their hearts pounding and adrenaline coursing through their veins, they plunged deep into the untamed wilderness, guided only by their unwavering belief in the riches that lay beneath the rugged terrain. The treacherous journey tested their mettle, but they remained undeterred, their eyes alight with the excitement of discovery. Equipped with nothing but their rusty picks and shovels with an unwavering spirit, they carved their path through the dense undergrowth, to mark out their plot undaunted by the dangers that lurked around every corner.

With just a small canvas tent pitched right outside the claim the pair had travelled through the vast wilderness, where untamed rivers rushed through rugged canyons and towering mountains stood as witnesses to their pursuit of the unknown. After tirelessly searching through the gold fields of California, their dreams of striking it rich were dwindling with every passing day. But then, like a beacon of hope, an opportunity presented itself - their last chance for fortune. As the days turned into nights and then back into days again, JD and Cole found themselves knee-deep in dirt they dreamt that a hidden fortune awaited them. It was whispered among winds that the land they traversed was indeed abundant with precious minerals and silver. However, the challenge lied not in knowing the existence of silver but in uncovering its elusive whereabouts.

JD and Cole ventured into the depths of the small hill, fuelled by their insatiable thirst for riches, As they progressed deeper, the realization dawned upon them - they needed reinforcements to keep the mine from crumbling under their feet, it was time to stop, As the day neared its end, they sought a respite and direction from Mr. Whiteoak himself. Their quest? To locate timber, a coveted resource amidst their desire to secure the mine. With spirits as high as the towering trees they sought, they eagerly approached Mr. Whiteoak's abode, hopeful for his wisdom and guidance. Greeted by his warm smile and wise demeanour, they wasted no time in presenting their inquiry, but he answered wasn't what they needed to hear, timber was sparse, As they found themselves in a vast, barren landscape devoid of any wood yard and sparsely populated by a meagre number of Mesquite trees or Prickly Ash. He suggested the pair would travel to Fort Worth and purchase from the Yard there, this was imported from different states was cheap enough, Fort Worth having a rail hub mainly for cattle but other supplies. their perseverance paid off, as they secured a stash of timber, enough to fill an entire wagon, Undeterred by the temporary setback that left them penniless, the next few weeks became an exhilarating task of survival. With no money to their name and only the shirts on their back, they embraced the thrill of the unknown, determined to strike silver in the face of adversity. Every day became an adventure, hunting for jack rabbit and other small mammals to survive in order to sustain their existence. Days turned into weeks as each day held the promise of both danger and glory.

As Mr. Whiteoak approached to check on the pair, his heart raced with anticipation, eager to witness firsthand the progress made by JD and Cole in the depths of the mine. The narrow tunnel seemed to stretch endlessly before him, its dark recesses shrouded in an air of mystery. As he ventured further, the sounds of their pounding pickaxes echoed in his ears, a symphony of determination mingled with anguish. The flickering glow of their lanterns cast dynamic shadows upon their weathered faces, etched with lines of sweat and determination. Mr. Whiteoak couldn't help but feel a surge of admiration for the resilience of these two young men to find their wealth. With each step deeper into the mine, he sensed the weight of their courageous endeavour pressing upon his own adventurous spirit, igniting a spark within him that yearned for exploration and conquest.

After acknowledging Mr Whiteoak, the three decided it was time for coffee, They headed back through the dark tunnel, as they turned around to retrace their steps, Cole's sharp eyes caught a fleeting glimpse of something unusual on the tunnel wall. Curiosity sparked within him, overshadowing the caffeine cravings momentarily. As Cole drew closer, the reflective surface revealed itself to be an intricately carved pattern, glimmering in the dim light. In that moment, he could feel their insatiable hunger for discovery intensify, He knew that this unexpected discovery of a small vein of silver could potentially unlock the gates to an entire realm of extraordinary wonders.

With a glint in his eye, he gripped his pick firmly and approached the rugged wall of earth. Determination coursed through his veins as he chipped away at the glistening vein, with Each strike of his tool echoed in the stillness as he delved deeper into the unknown, embracing the thrill of discovery. The air was thick with anticipation, and he couldn't help but feel an adrenaline-fueled rush. Mr. Whiteoak watched in awe as JD and Cole uncovered their long-awaited treasure, 'Silver'. It was a moment of triumph that felt like the culmination of a lifetime of daring escapades.

The following day, Cole's heart was pounding and a sense of excitement in his veins, Cole hopped onto his trusty steed. The sun was shining brightly overhead, promising a day ripe with adventure. Clutching a small bag of silver ore tightly in his hand, he set off towards Fort Worth, determined to find the assay office. Each galloping step of his horse filled him with a rush of adrenaline. With a heart full of anticipation, he presented the precious silver ore he had worked tirelessly to mine. As the authenticity of the gleaming silver was confirmed, a thrill of excitement coursed through his veins. With a mixture of satisfaction and a pinch of nervousness, he entered into negotiations, carefully weighing the value of the hard-earned treasure. Eventually, the deal was struck, as he proudly sold the ore an overwhelming sense of relief washed over him, Their grand plan was about to unfold as it was time that they eagerly sent for their wives, their partners in crime, to join them in their pursuit of a brighter future. The promise of new beginnings and limitless possibilities filled the air, fuelling their determination and courage. With every plank they laid and every beam they raised; they were building not just a physical structure but a haven for their loved ones.

Several months had past, and it wasn't long before word got out and people started to arrive in the area, Mr Atwal asked Tony to manage the situation, and before long a small encampment had started to grow, Tony and Mr Atwal were delighted as the amount of cash it was bringing in. As the sun dipped below the horizon, painting the sky with hues of orange and pink, the camp transformed into something more than just a gathering of tents. It evolved into a bustling small frontier town, pulsating with energy and anticipation. The campfire crackled, casting a warm glow that enticed both weary travellers and fearless adventurers alike. The once barren landscape now boasted buildings that sprouted like wildflowers. Whiteoak Springs was born, it was named after the creek but really was after Tony. A year had passed, Showcasing remarkable growth and development.

What was once merely a humble gathering of tents and crude shelters now boasting a diverse array of structures, symbolizing progress, and ambition. Sturdy log cabins lined the streets, their chimneys puffing gentle plumes of smoke into the crisp air. A beating heart of the community, bustling with activity day and night. The once barren landscape had undergone a remarkable transformation to a Saloon, The Mine, Stenson Ranch, General Store, Undertakers, Brothel, Apothecary, US Marshal, Sheriff, Barbers, Doctor, Cattle Company, Bank, Court House and many more, Just a few examples of the bustling town's burgeoning enterprises. As the small frontier town continued to thrive, its residents revelled in a sense of accomplishment, their hard work and shared vision bearing fruit for all to see. With a population blooming to 44, this thriving little place with attracted more trouble than it is worth. Lying near the main cattle route from New Mexico through to Fort Worth and a trail from the Pan Handle, An influx of people brought forth the unwanted lawless, a wide spectrum, from street sellers seeking their fortunes to industrious ranch hands searching for employment opportunities. However, the allure of this gathering also enticed a less desirable faction, comprised of street urchins, vagrants, outlaws, and opportunists. In the face of this heterogeneous mix, it became evident that the event's reputation as a magnet for individuals of all walks of life carried both positive and negative implications. While the presence of resourceful individuals seeking legitimate economic prospects brought promise to the occasion, the unsavoury elements that took advantage of the opportunity presented a challenge that needed to be addressed with prudence and discernment..

All looking for a quick buck. Tony and Mr Atwal now had their work cut out, they appointed Marshal Chapman then Sheriff Smiff, then later two Texas Rangers Soapy and Poncho joined the law enforcement team. Tony soon saw the opportunity to open a Gunsmiths in the growing town. Buildings had started to be erected at an alarming rate. Mr Atwal being voted in as Governor of Stenson, Although he owned most of the land, This is a small county within the State of Texas, Times were difficult as the war had taken its toll within small areas and there were still pockets of resistance against the federal government, Small settlements like Whiteoak Springs found the benefits and opportunities for business, and opportunities to grow which offered many to prosper. With this, he found people nominating him as a suitable candidate for presidency, but he declined and settled to continue as governor. Mr Atwal helped President Grant on a number reform issues, including presidents' administration that prosecuted Mormon polygamists and vice crimes like pornography and abortion. With the nation gripped by a severe economic depression and financial crisis, the current state of affairs demands our utmost attention and expertise. Despite recent setbacks, the Republican Party continues to maintain the support of Mr. Atwal. While disagreements within the party have become more pronounced, Mr. Atwal's allegiance underscores the enduring backing that the Republicans enjoyed.

Chapter 4

The Ladies of Whiteoak's (Temperance Society)

In the early days of Whiteoak's, a bustling and tight-knit community, the town's esteemed ladies congregated for a grand tea party to launch the highly anticipated Whiteoak's Temperance Society. This extravagant gathering unfolded in an atmosphere of utmost opulence, as elegant table settings adorned with delicate bone-China and gleaming silverware set the stage for a refined afternoon. The air was filled with laughter and animated conversations as the ladies, draped in luxurious silk gowns and adorned with dazzling jewellery, sipped their fragrant teas from porcelain cups. As they indulged in delectable pastries and finger sandwiches, the ladies exchanged stories and shared their visions for a town free from the vices of alcohol and Ms Kittys establishment of ill repute. Among the distinguished attendees were a multitude of remarkable Ladies, exemplifying the utmost elegance and poise. Notable figures in attendance included the revered preacher's wife, Tan, distinguished Mrs P, Caroline from the esteemed bank, the impeccable Dolly, the School mistress, the resourceful Sue from the Fur traders, and the illustrious Olive. The soirée was further graced by the presence of Lady Eva Fouquet, the elegant and influential Ms Kate, and many other remarkable individuals. As for the men of the town, they were left to their own devices, their absence on this occasion accentuating the prominence of the powerful and inspiring women in this community. But mischievous bad boy Willis, infamous for his drunken escapades, had meticulously crafted plans to utterly disrupt the occasion. With boldness fuelling his mischievous spirit,

Willis sought to shatter the tranquil atmosphere, injecting chaos and uproar where it was least expected. Armed with his inexhaustible wit and a knack for pushing boundaries, he strategized how to leave a lasting impact on this otherwise harmonious event. He hatched a cunning plan, devising a surprising disguise that would stir up the event and reveal the clandestine machinations of the womenfolk.

He persuaded Chapper's, Who would later to become the town Marshal, to don a woman's dress, aiming to infiltrate the harmonious occasion and unveil the secrets concealed within their whispered conversations. The sight of Chapper's, donning a woman's dress and blouse, topped off with a fanciful filly hat, elicited roars of laughter from the town's men. As if playing a prank on reality itself, Chapper's bold sartorial choice became an instant source of amusement for those fortunate enough to witness the spectacle. With each giggle and guffaw, it was clear that the residents of this small town revelled in the whimsy and absurdity presented before them. Chapper's, unapologetically daring to challenge gender norms, had inadvertently become the unexpected source of comic relief, sparking infectious witticism amidst the otherwise mundane day-to-day. The perfect plan to enter the lady's tea party of Whiteoak's Temperance Society, As they approached the door, Willis's unwavering demeanour seemed to say, "Nothing can stand in our way." With a firm hand on the doorknob, he swung it open, there stood Chapper's, dolled up in a rather amusing getup. Picture this: a mishmash of female attire, from dresses to blouses, all topped off with a whimsical filly hat. It was a sight that couldn't help but elicit a friendly chuckle. One had to appreciate Chapper's boldness and sense of humour, that was it.

The ladies of Whiteoak's Temperance Society took no time at all to recognize Chapper's and they had completely foiled Willis' scheme. Oh, the audacity of his misguided intentions! They could hardly contain their mirth as they witnessed the spectacle before them. It was an uproarious display, one that threatened to send them tumbling off their chairs in fits of uncontrollable laughter. The sheer absurdity of the scene was simply too much to bear, and their witty tongues danced with delight as they exchanged knowing glances. Every exaggerated gesture, every comedic twist of fate.

Lady Eva Fouquet, the indomitable force of wit and charm, orchestrated a grand spectacle that reverberated through the entire town. she swiftly outmanoeuvred the two mischievous rascals, leaving them no choice but to flee, tails literally tucked between their legs. As the echoes of laughter filled the air, not only from the ladies but with the town's men, Chapper's fled to his encampment on the outskirts of town and quickly changed back into his normal attire, but with a heavy weight of embarrassment, Bad boy Willis was nowhere to be seen, he had disappeared, but he was later seen leaving the Saloon drunk as a skunk as if nothing had happened. As Chapper's continued through the day his embarrassment of the event was still present. The local Gazette printed an article on the day's proceedings, the town still chuckles when it reflects on that fateful, humorous day. It's as if the memory is etched with a twinkle in its eye, grinning from ear to ear, recounting the hilarious mishaps that unfolded that afternoon.

As time continued its steady march forward, a captivating turn of events unfolded. In an audacious twist of fate, the ladies, with their fiery determination, decided to exact their well-deserved revenge on the men. And later that month, just as the anticipation reached its peak, an exhilarating announcement swept through the town. Chapper's, now a town's resident, was offered the prestigious role of Marshal. The day of the Marshals swearing in, before the Judge and the Town Mayor, this momentous event wasn't without its fair share of controversy. The air was thick with excitement as the new Marshal prepared to take his oath. But in true adventurous fashion, a sudden commotion erupted, throwing the ceremony into disarray. Rumours flew through the crowd including the ladies of the Temperance, adding an extra layer of intrigue to the already tense atmosphere. Yet, amidst the chaos, As the Marshal stood undeterred, two cowhands known as members of the notorious Oaks Gang embarked on a mischievous mission to cause mayhem and chaos during the ceremony, With their trusty spurs jingling and hats tilted at a rakish angle, their adventurous spirits propelled them forward, ready to leave their mark on then the lawless town with their six shooters, pointed at the Marshal ready to perform an assassination, but the Mayor and the Marshal were quick to recognise the situation, And end the chaos as their exploits was flawed, The cowhands retreated to the shadows leaving Justice back to the streets.

 As the day went on, the air was thick with excitement and intrigue as Chapper's newfound opportunity unfolded before everyone's admiring eye, the men hatched a plan to indulge in an unforgettable afternoon of wine and port. Setting the stage for an epic gathering, they laid out an enticing array of velvety reds and rich fortified wines from far-off lands followed by imported cheeses. They revelled in the anticipation of discovering hidden gems and marvelled at the prospect of a taste buds' journey through different countries. As each bottle was uncorked, the room filled with a symphony of laughter and animated conversations. As the men raised their glasses, the clinking sound filled the air, echoing the excitement that pulsed through the room. They were toasting Chapper's new position, celebrating his bravery in taking on this new adventure.

Outside the window of the saloon, their adventurous spirits were met with a sight that further fuelled their adrenaline. A vibrant crowd had gathered, wielding colourful banners and rhythmic tambourines. It was the Whiteoak's Temperance Society, a group of intrepid souls dedicated to exploring uncharted territories of sobriety, Singing hymns, and protesting against alcohol, The Marshal wasted no time in attempting to disperse the unruly crowd, but their adventurous spirit driving them to take immediate action.

However, the ladies proved to be quite stubborn, unyielding in their resolve to maintain their presence amidst the chaos. So, he decided to let them have their day, as soon as they had arrived it seemed they had left, and there was peace again in the main street of Whiteoak's. Their voices could be heard in the distance winds, and this was an eventful day indeed for all.

The ladies of our community truly exemplify resourcefulness by organizing events such as craft afternoons, accompanied by delightful servings of tea and other delectable fancies, beckoning the ladies to indulge in their flavoursome charms. As they mingle and share stories, the atmosphere is further enlivened by the presence of distinguished guest speakers, who grace us with their wisdom and expertise. Their eloquent speeches captivate them, transporting them to distant realms of knowledge and inspiration.

Over December and January, last year, The Ladies of Whiteoak's Temperance Society took a stand against the sale of liquor by organizing a peaceful protest outside the Painted Pony Saloon on Main Street. With unwavering determination, they sought to bring attention to the social and health consequences associated with alcohol consumption. Dressed in their finest attire, the ladies displayed unity and grace as they advocated for a ban on liquor sales.. The message read "Lips that Touch Liquor shall not touch ours" may seem quite straightforward, but let's not forget that everyone is entitled to their own opinions and beliefs. While the sentiment behind it might be fuelled by good intentions, it's important to remember that individuals have different views when it comes to alcohol consumption. It's possible that those who proposed this idea may have concerns about the potential negative effects of alcohol. However, it's also worth noting that husbands or partners might have their own perspectives on the matter.

April, saw the ladies of the Temperance society busy again. Ready to announce that they will be having another guest speaker held in the Court House. A Social reformer had been invited to provide propriety and encomium in her speech. Country wide the Temperance Society is now boasting 22.000 members. This meeting will cover of the existence and seriousness of the disease of alcoholism and how to prove the efficacy of asylum treatments for alcoholics. But this was dampened after Mrs Chapman the Marshal's wife had been looking for the Marshal with a telegram from Fort Worth, With news about Ms Kitty's place from the district Judges office, She entered the Saloon expecting to find him at his usual spot, The Saloon is not a place for ladies of social standing or of etiquette, quite a commotion took place with whiskey and other Liquor flowing with great merriment after several hours. As the Marshal entered the Saloon unaware that his wife was in there, only to find her drunk as a skunk and very intoxicated dancing, flirting with the cowhands causing quite a stir, not a great advert for the Temperance Society. Normally the Marshal calls in for a drink and a game of poker before he heads home. But the Town Mayor and the Marshal had to escort the Marshal's wife home before any more embarrassment could occur, I must add, the following day Mrs Chapman wasn't seen through the town as she normally would, As she was possibly too embarrassed for her behaviour. Again, this was not uncommon as the Preachers wife had a similar experience.

The Whiteoak's Chapel was going to host an Easter parade through the town on Easter Sunday in conjunction with the Temperance society, but unfortunate events left the preacher rather embarrassed. The preacher's wife had been known to like a tipple or two and was rather intoxicated, that particular evening, She had fallen over from outside the Saloon with her britches around her ankles making rather a spectacle of herself. This left most of her modesty showing, which was very unchristian like. Some cowhands in the saloon and one or two passers-by jeered at the spectacle and mocked the situation. Sadly, the following Sunday service at the Chapel was very short of attendants which left the preacher no choice on cancelling the parade out of embarrassment.

Another was Ms Mags of the Haberdashery; she was arrested for being drunk and causing damage to Whiteoak's property. Sheriff Smiff had arrested her and sent her before the Judge. As the Court session re-adjourned shortly after lunchtime. Marshal Chapman called for the Witnesses and the evidence to be presented to Judge Pee. After they announced the verdict as guilty, The Judge passed sentence of 2 days in Jail to sober up and pay court costs.

But from these little strays of mishaps, they are all forgiven, and the ladies of Whiteoak's Temperance Society continue in their united mission with a warm and friendly spirit. Their dedication to promoting sobriety and ensuring the well-being of their community shines through every endeavour they undertake. Whiteoak's Temperance Society truly knows how to keep its members engaged and entertained throughout the year. Their vibrant calendar of events is a testament to their dedication and passion.

Chapter 5

Walk With The Marshal:

Its early morning and Marshal Chapman is greeted by Sheriff Smiff making his way towards the courthouse, he was pleasantly surprised to see him give a warm greeting, normally it's about some event or a petty criminal that had evaded him. The air was filled with a sense of camaraderie as the two law enforcement officers exchanged friendly smiles and a firm handshake, as the day's work had begun, Despite the heavy clouds hanging in the air, it was a surprisingly uplifting atmosphere on this dull day. As the Marshal gazed down Main Street, a sense of tranquillity seemed to permeate the surroundings. People were strolling leisurely, their faces illuminated by genuine smiles. It was as if the overcast sky had failed to dampen their spirits. Perhaps it was the knowledge that even amidst an uneventful day, there was still joyed to be found in the simplest of things, As he stepped out of his porch on to the main street, a wave of delightful aroma reached his nostrils. The rich, invigorating scent of freshly brewed coffee enveloped him, instantly waking up his senses. He couldn't help but smile, knowing that his neighbour Dodger, the friendly local undertaker was always diligent in his craft, The relaxed pace at which Dodger was making caskets seemed to match perfectly with the serene ambiance of the neighbourhood, as if time itself was following the comforting rhythm of that first cup of coffee. Ever since Ms Kitty's, the bustling house of ill repute and hotspot for entertainment had closed down, this part of town has notably become more serene and tranquil.

The Marshal started to walk and do his rounds with a relaxed swagger. The weight of his responsibilities seemed to lighten with each step, allowing him to breathe in the crisp morning air and take in the quietude of the town awakening. The familiar faces of the townsfolk greeted him as they hastily went about their daily routines, preparing for the day ahead. With a nod here and a friendly smile there, the Marshal exchanged pleasantries, making sure to acknowledge each person he encountered.

Ms. Kate bustled about in front of the Mercantile, hastily preparing the vibrant array of fresh produce. Her nimble hands prepared plump fresh rabbit and fresh daily bread, as the inviting scent of nature's bounty filled the air. Meanwhile, at a nearby bench, Bubba sat leisurely puffing on his smoke, savouring the tranquillity of the moment. The relaxed tempo of the scene seemed to harmonize with the unhurried pace of small-town life, creating an atmosphere where time stood still. With a relaxed smile on the Marshal's face, he warmly acknowledged the two familiar faces.

Standing on his porch, Marshal, a regular customer, strolled by and exchanged a brief chat with Mr Whiteoak. The air was filled with a sense of camaraderie and community, as both men shared stories and laughed together for a short time, Marie, Mr Whiteoak's partner, a horse trader and dealer sat listening to the pair. As the Marshal continued on his way, his gaze shifted towards the old undertaker's building, standing there empty and worn down. Despite its state of dilapidation, there was a certain charm to its weathered appearance. The peeling paint and cracked windows spoke of a time gone by, carrying memories of long-forgotten stories within its walls, as if the building held the stories of a multitude of lives, whispering in the wind to anyone who cared to listen, a silent sentinel, a reminder of the passage of time and the tales long told.

In the brisk morning air, the diligent Marshal could discern the distant sound of the school bell resounding through the surroundings. The melodic chimes, fused with the voice of Ms. Dolly, served as a welcoming call for the eager children to gather for yet another day of learning at school. As the bell continued to resonate through the air, he couldn't help but reflect on the importance of education and the impact it had on shaping future generations.

The Marshal continued to proceed to greet the townsfolk, Mr. Thomas a distinguished gentleman comfortably settled on his porch, his heart at ease, a steaming cup of fresh brewed tea in one hand, and a well-worn pipe in the other. The air, filled with a sense of calm, embraced his idyllic routine. Meanwhile, Mrs. P, an impeccably professional and diligent woman, performed her daily ritual of unlocking the doors to the bank, preparing it for the customers eagerly awaiting its services.

Opposite, Red and Reno eagerly received a pristine shipment of pelts, ready to embark on the next phase of their entrepreneurial journey, Sue, Red's wife, meticulously scrutinized each pelt, ensuring its impeccable quality. With her discerning eye and commitment to excellence, Sue play's a crucial role in maintaining the high standards. As the Marshal passed by, Red gave a subtle nod to acknowledge his presence. This simple gesture carried a weight of respect.

As the Marshal ambled along, his steps came to a halt as he reached the trio of buildings. They're stood Mr J Boxx, the Registrar and Proprietor of the Assay Office, engaged in an animated discussion with his partner Lady Eva Fouquet. Nearby, Jeb and Olive from the Apothecary were deeply engrossed in conversation debating which herbs to collect next. It was evident that the atmosphere was relaxed and leisurely, as the group exchanged laughter and anecdotes. Next door to the Assay Office, Franco sat back in his chair, relishing every sip of his morning coffee. As the rich aroma filled the room, Meanwhile, his wife, Filomena diligently went about her tasks, armed with a determined focus. The sound of her sweeping and cleaning echoed faintly through the walls, adding a subtle rhythm to the peaceful atmosphere. As the barbershop was near to open, a few early-morning customers patiently waiting for a fresh haircut and beard trim. Marshal Chapman, with his signature relaxed demeanour, greeted each and every one of them with a warm smile.

At the end of the street, with its vibrant sign illuminating the morning sky, stood the Painted Pony Saloon. JP his diligent hands meticulously swept away the remnants of the previous night's revelry with a hint of stale tobacco and spilt whiskey. Inside, the atmosphere was filled with a subtle hum of anticipation, As the working girls and JP prepared for another day and evening, there was a palpable sense of calm and ease in the air. The atmosphere was relaxed, as if everyone had settled into a familiar rhythm. The working girls took their time getting ready, They exchanged playful banter and laughter, sharing stories from the previous night's clientele. The Marshal, stopped at Lincoln corner, were the Wells Fargo & Co, Pony Express is, with its weathered wooden walls, adorned with a colourful sign, seemed to tell stories of a bygone era. It was as if time itself had slowed down amidst the creaking of floorboards and the gentle rustle of papers inside. The Marshal found solace in the simplicity of this place.

Andrea, the friendly Post Mistress, greeted him with a warm smile and asked if there was any new post to be sent, he simply replied none today thank you, While on the corner his keen eyes caught sight of Martin known as 'Wonbag,' Andrea's husband, and the Coach Master, preparing to swap out the tired horses from the recently arrived coach. With a friendly grin, the Marshal approached him, offering a helping hand with a light-hearted exchange of anecdotes and laughter, Martin accepted his help, the pair quickly changed the exhausted horses, ensuring that the coach remains in prime condition for its next journey.

The Marshal moved on, his gaze shifted towards his left, the gleaming white church spire stood tall and proud, untouched by the passage of years. Standing beside it, the Preacher Mark exuded an air of professionalism. His presence was commanding, his voice steady, as he spoke of faith and hope to a small group of miners before they entered the Mine, With every word, he instilled a sense of reverence and inspiration like a protective shield against the unknown dangers lurking within the depths of the mine. Meanwhile, just a few steps away, his wife Tan diligently swept their porch, a silent testament to the unwavering support they both offered to those brave souls embarking on their perilous day. Next to the Church was a small track way, this is called Belle End, this is where the Haberdashery is, Arthur, also known as 'Trailer,' With a steaming cup of coffee in hand, Arthur's relaxed posture epitomizes the peace that comes with a lifetime of hard work, His wife Mag's offers a time-honoured craft that encompasses the art of outfitting individuals with the finest accessories and essentials for their wardrobes.

Beyond The Haberdashery is the Fields, The Texas Rangers Office which also plays a pivotal role in upholding law enforcement in the region. Poncho, with his sharp instincts and astute investigative skills, has successfully cracked numerous complex cases. Soapy, on the other hand, showcases exceptional aptitude in forensic analysis, leaving no trail unexplored. Together, they form an indispensable duo, complimenting each other's strengths and serving as an embodiment of the Rangers', The Marshal is always thankful for their help, dedicated as they work tirelessly to uphold the law and ensure peace and justice in the community.

The Shoeshine Shack is just near the wood yard, Blue Eyes and Creature Moonshine, In a daring escape from the clutches of a cruel stepmother, a brave brother and sister mustered up the courage to embark on a treacherous journey away from home. Determined to leave behind the beatings and hardships, they set off into the unknown, facing countless trials along the way. As young, vulnerable souls, they battled hunger and exhaustion, their mere survival hanging by a thread. Each passing day brought new challenges, including the ever-present danger of falling into the hands of unforgiving Indians. Yet, against all odds, luck smiled upon them, leading them to stumble upon their saving grace: Whiteoak Springs. Desperate, hungry and in rags, they were given a hot meal by Mrs P, The Governor and Mr Whiteoak took pity and agreed they could stay and renovate a small chicken shack to call their home, they were given a chance to develop a shoe-shining business which became successful, this is to fund their existence in the town, The Children are now schooled by Ms Dolly and town folk always look out for their welfare as they continue with their young adventure. Since their first day they have thrived at Whiteoak's and are well looked after. The Marshal always checks in on these Children but this particular time he knew they were making their way to the School house.

As the Marshal turns and strides past the Mine and Miners office, a familiar face greets him: Mr. C Rayburn. With a friendly tone of voice, Mr. C Rayburn warmly welcomes the Marshal and engages in casual conversation of yesterday's topics from the Gazette, then invites him to a coffee, The Marshal declines, then as he finishes his conversation with Mr C Rayburn, but his attention was caught by Big Sam, he noticed the blacksmith in his element, hammering away at the forge, shaping solid steel with skilful precision. The rhythmic clinking of metal against metal echoed through the air, creating a symphony of craftsmanship. Each strike seemed purposeful, energy and expertise fused into every blow. Big Sam's strong hands moved with both grace and power, a testament to his years of experience As he watched the blacksmith expertly fashion horseshoes, tools, and other implements, he marvelled at the skill and dedication it took to create such practical and essential items. Sitting on the Blacksmith's porch was Jackie his wife, as she sat on the worn wooden porch in her favourite chair, her spectacles perched on her nose, Jackie engrossed herself in the pages of the local Gazette. The gentle breeze rustled the pages, causing her hair to dance ever so lightly. It was a picturesque moment, where the simple pleasure of absorbing stories and news came alive in their cozy corner. The Marshal greeted them both with just a smile and a tip of his hat.

As he walked past the quaint saddlery next door, a small smile curved his lips as he noticed Monty and Mags. Monty, A skilled saddler with his weathered hands and a twinkle in his eyes that spoke of years of craftsmanship. Putting out his latest hand-crafted wears for display, Mags, his loyal wife, ever-present by his side, A fragrance of high-quality leather permeated the air along with the smell of the forge next door, again he greeted them both with just a smile and a tip of his hat. Outside the courthouse, Sheriff Smiff leaned against the wall, a picture of calm and patience as he waited for the Marshal to arrive for the morning sessions with Judge Pee, Sheriff Smiff's laid-back demeanour belied the gravity of his duties, but his years of experience had taught him the importance of maintaining a sense of calm in the face of legal proceedings. At the Court House, there resided Judge Pee, along with her husband "Lawdog". Their presence in the legal realm brought a sense of dedication and authority. Judge Pee is one tough cookie. Renowned for her no-nonsense approach, she didn't spare anyone from the consequences of their actions. Her reputation preceded her, and defendants and attorneys alike knew they were in for a challenging battle when appearing in her courtroom.

The morning proceedings swiftly came to an end, the Marshal embarked on the rest of his journey through the quaint town. Passing past the old Doc's Building were newcomers Mose and Lil sat on the porch drinking their coffee watching the daily life pass by, The Marshal bid them a good Morning and continued with a relaxed pace, he caught sight of a group of Cowhands on horseback, representing the renowned Triple 'R' Cattle Company. Their confident presence in the town reaffirmed the Marshal's belief in the local ranching community's diligent work, these men were just about to ride out with fresh instruction from Jim, Bob and Ralf the owners of the Triple 'R' Cattle Company.

The Marshal made his way back towards his own office. The Governors Building, a grand and impressive single-story structure, stood as a symbol of authority and governance. Before departing, the Governor took a moment to greet the Marshal, acknowledging the importance of his position with a handshake and smile. After a Morning of greeting and interacting with the townsfolk, the Marshal finally found himself back in the familiar confines of his own office. The sense of accomplishment washed over him, a long-awaited coffee has finally arrived from his wife, delicately brewed to perfection. Its rich aroma filled the air of his office, this left the Marshal with a content smile on his face.

Chapter 6

Deputy Tate:

It was late afternoon, A young man pulled out the gun out of the holster in one swift motion. It's an easy thing to do because I've done it hundreds of times in practice. The weight is right, the balance perfect. The cold steel of the barrel rests comfortably in my palm. I'm so familiar with it that I don't even have to think about what I'm doing. The sound is a release of power, a small explosion. I know how much energy is in the tiny cartridge, and how the energy is transformed when the cartridge hits the wall or ground. It's like a little lightning bolt going off, a tiny thunderstorm, and when you point the gun at someone, The sound reverberates through the room, and when it stops, everyone is quiet. Everyone is watching you. I didn't have to say a word. I don't need to explain anything. The man opposite me was dead, and it was time to claim the reward, one bystander said "You're gonna make a good sheriff kid," I lowered my gun and slid it back into the holster. There is still some tension in the air, but people are smiling. They're happy to see I have just gunned down a notorious outlaw. After handing him in at the Sheriff's Office and collecting the reward, I made my way back to the saloon, I felt like a million dollars but with some sadness as I've just taken someone's life! I ask the Bar Keep if there are any rooms for rent for the evening, he smiles and said "Yes," I smile back and said, "I'll take it," I made my way upstairs, to find the room, It's a small room, and there's only a single bed, It's dull and dark with only a candle for light but I don't mind. A few minutes later a knock on the door, I said "enter", A girl walks in and sits on the edge of the bed she then asks "is there anything I can do for you, would you like a little company for the evening mister," I know that the girl is a working girl, I had just been paid for a bounty, I declined and asked the girl to leave, its wasn't time for pleasure just yet, I knew that another bounty was just outside of Whiteoak's, and I needed my rest and wits about me for the following day. I spent the next day walking around town, talking to people trying to find out if there was a hideout. slowly getting used to the fact that people are now coming up to me and not treating me like a stranger, It feels a bit strange, I headed out of town towards the place known as 'Deadman's finger' the first place to look for my next bounty. A chap near the gunsmith said it was a good place to hide as in the early days it was rumoured a gang of partisan raiders wintered there, It's a group of rocks and a ravine about 13 miles from Whiteoak's, I was new to these parts, as I grew up near Fort Worth, I rode about four hours without any joy, So I headed back to Whiteoak's, I hitched my horse up to the hitching post and entered the Marshal's Office, Marshal Chapman, He seemed a quiet fellow and easy to talk to, We chatted for a while and I explained I didn't manage to find the next bounty, He said "don't worry Kid," there's always another day, He then asked for my name, I replied "Tate," I explained that I was from a small place near Fort Worth, After a while he then offered me a Job as Deputy Marshal. He explained it had been vacant for some time as Sheriff Smiff was voted the Town Sheriff and left the position, This couldn't have come at a better time. Marshal Chapman said, "The pay isn't great but it's a regular job and you'll do well." The next morning, I headed back to the office, getting ready for another day. I was just about to start organizing the paperwork when the Office door flies open. "You the new sheriff?" grunted a man "No," I replied "Deputy Marshal," I was holding the office while Marshal Chapman was visiting Sheriff Smiff. I looked up and saw a big burly man standing in the doorway.

He was wearing a red shirt, torn pants, and a brown vest. His boots are scuffed, and his hair is shaggy and unkept, his beard was matted. He was also holding an old pistol in his hand. "You know who I am?" he said, I replied "No," Suddenly my mouth went dry, and my heart started to race, "I'm Big Red Bill. And I hear your looking for me, I replied, "Yeah." then I hesitated, As I rose from the chair I started to get clammy and replied, "Okay, come on in." He steps into the office cautiously and takes a seat still with the pistol in his hand. I said to him "I heard you was good with a gun." "Yeah, I guess." said Red Bill, "Let's see what you got." I drew quickly and asked him to drop it, I was quicker than him he didn't have time to lift the pistol from his lap, By this time Marshal Chapman walks through the door way, he said "Hell Kid, who have you got here," I replied 'Big Red Bill wanted for rustling," I slowly showed the Marshal his wanted poster from the other side of the desk still pointing my pistol at him, The Marshal said " Well done Tate, Sheriff Smiff had been looking for this one for three months," He soon disarmed Big Red Bill, I was quite relieved as Marshal Chapman then took him across to the Jail.

I needed a drink my throat was like the desert on a hot day, That could have gone bad, and my adrenalin was high. Marshal Chapman came back after a short while and said "Coffee Tate," "yes," I replied still with a dryness to my voice, come on I'll treat you to some of Mrs P's biscuits & coffee. The rest of the day was quite dull, Just hanging around the office. Marshal Chapman asked if I was fixed up for a place to stay, I said I was renting a room in the Saloon, he replied, "no kid don't stop there," Go to the Governors building there is a room for rent there, You won't get interrupted by the soiled doves after your hard earnt cash. I headed off to the Governors building, Met with the lady that runs the rent book, and paid-up front for a month. Marshal Chapman was right; It was much nicer than the rooms in the Saloon. A week or so had gone by, I was settling into my new job. Marshal Chapman showed me how to deal with the paperwork, but it was nearly time to go, This time out with Marshal Chapman, first to Fort Worth to collect the latest dispatches and warrants from the District Judges Office, then to supply ourselves to find another outlaw. My mouth was dry again but felt an excitement, I asked, "when do we leave," Marshal replied, "early in the morning Kid".

The next morning, I woke excited but a little apprehensive as it was my first time out with Marshal Chapman, I went over to the Livery to saddle the horses, then met Marshal Chapman outside his Office, we only had 4 days provisions.

"Morning kid," Said the Marshal "let's get going," it was early, the sun had just rose and not many people were about in town. "Yarh" a kick of the heels and we were off, heading north to Fort Worth, As we made our way out of town, Marshal Chapman was quiet for the first few miles, but I guess he wasn't a morning chap, As we made our way, the Marshal told me some stories of his early years in the Army, he was a tough man, but had a good heart. Trail was easy to follow as tracks had been made by many wagons going back a forth, Whiteoak's received a monthly supply wagon from Fort Worth, If the town prospers enough the town Mayor and the Governor hope that the railroad would pass through one day, but for now they rely on the supply wagon. A mail coach stops and waters at the springs then changes horses at the Pony Express office on Lincoln corner. We rode for around 25 miles, then Marshal Chapman suggested we rested the horses for a while, we dismounted and walked, the horses grazing when they could, this was a rugged environment. We walked for a few miles then the Marshal said, "hold on, wait here kid," I had no idea what he was doing, he wondered off the trail after a few minutes he shouted, "Over here kid," I walked over to his position, "Look" he said lying on the ground was a dead Injun and many horse tracks, I said "What we goin' to do with that dead Injun," Marshal replied "Leave him." And again, he said, "Leave him," his voice was low and tired. The old man's words grated on his raw nerves, which meant only one thing, he didn't not want to think about Indians, their ways, their habits, or their death, as for the Marshal he fought them for many years and seen enough blood shed for one man's lifetime.

The Marshal looked like his mind was numb, and he suddenly looked tired. He said, "Tate I'm tired of this, of all of it." I didn't know what to say back to him you could clearly see he was troubled. We mounted and started to ride again, I said, "who did this?" the Marshal replied, "probably a revenge killing for the sheep herders a few weeks back. The buzzards and the coyotes are his comfort now, kid." We rode for a while I asked Marshal Chapman why he was like that, He said he hunted them the with army, and had many encounters with them, He then explained they killed all his wife's family on a raid and if it wasn't for the patrol he was on, he wouldn't have been able to save his wife. I didn't ask anymore, he was quiet for a while as we rode until it was nearly dusk, he said, "Over here Kid there's a good place to set up camp and rest the horses." We unsaddled the horses, then made a fire, we sat for a while then brewed a coffee, The Marshal fixed up some salt pork and biscuits, It was a clear night not a cloud in sight, Marshal soon lent his head against the saddle, then threw his blanket over and he was then off to sleep, I kept watch for an hour or so then we swapped over, Not before long it was dawn the sun was rising with a fresh mist in the air. "Coffee," Said the Marshal I replied "Yes," after a while we saddled up and we were on our way again. As we rode for a few more miles we saw a dust cloud, Marshal said, "Don't worry Kid," It's only the wagon supply on its way through to Whiteoak's, The Marshal rode off ahead to meet up with the Wagon, The Driver and a man with a shotgun sat next to him, They chatted for a while as I caught up, The man with the gun said, "Morning young man, so you're the new kid that gunned down Finn" I replied, "I guess so," he then went on the say he deserved everything he had coming to him and then thanked me, He said to the Marshal, "look after this one," The marshal tipped his brim on his hat, and replied "yes sir"! time to go Kid, We weren't far from Fort Worth, The Marshal explained I was to report to the District Judges Office, After we had ridden into town and tied our horses up at the stables. The Marshal had business elsewhere, he followed on and said he would meet me at the Office as he wouldn't be very long. I walked along the street, the street was bustling with life, people, carts, wagons and horses everywhere, I got to the District Judge's office, I opened the door and a large man very well dressed, with a limp, a rugged face with a scar to the left cheek greeted me, I explained I was deputy Marshal Tate from Whiteoak's and the

Marshal wouldn't be long, The man looked me up and down then said, "So you're a deputy Marshal?, More like two streaks of bacon." He turned and went out of the door, I thought how rude of this gentleman, I stood for a while then knocked on the Judges Door but no reply, I waited for a while then the man with a limp returned with Marshal Chapman, I must have looked puzzled, The Marshal said let me introduce you to the District Judge, I was in disbelief, but we both went into his office, the Judge had a mannerism of unkindness towards me, Then asked us to sit down.

The District Judge didn't seem to be a gentleman, his rugged voice and scars said something different, but you could clearly see he was a well-educated man. He told the Marshal that I was to stay at Fort Worth for a while and he had a mission for me later in the week, My emotions were a little mixed, I had relied on my instincts and the advice from Marshal Chapman, Fort Worth was a much larger town than I remembered, After the Judge had handed the latest dispatches and warrants we both left the Office. I said to Marshal Chapman, "What kinda man is the Judge," He replied, "the man you want on your side." He then reassured me, and then said everything would be ok, there's a small café down on the next street, we will grab a beer and a steak before we leave and it's on me, He then explained, that there was a cattle drive due in with two outlaws, The Judge requested for you, as you have taken in two real bad men on your first week as Deputy, I still wasn't sure but I was looking forward to the steak. We both sat down in the café and ordered, the Marshal then told me he had paid for a room for me for a month, and after the two outlaws had been caught, Then I was to return to Whiteoak's, then he finished his steak and he left. I was on my own from now until the job had been done.

The Marshal had already paid, and I left shortly after to find my room, he said it was a boarding house not far from the District Judges Office, It wasn't long before I found the house, my room was small and dark, with a single bed and a small dressing table with a wash basin and jug, a wardrobe next to the bed which was empty and a small table with an oil lamp on it, It had a small window looking onto the street which let light in, A luxury as most, are very dark and situated at the back of the buildings. I had a few days to explore as I hadn't been to town for a long time since my folks had passed, There was a large number of saloons, boarding houses, brothels, gambling parlours and hotels, as well as a small assortment of mercantile businesses between the Courthouse Square and the railroad depot, these are mainly brick and wooden buildings, These had all opened since I was last here, I was informed that Hell's Half Acre was a rough and rowdy precinct of Fort Worth and that's why the Judge requested me to help, I decided to go to the gathering place for townspeople, farmers and cattlemen where they buy food, gear, or items in bulk for long trips on the trail, The general store, this is often the town's post office, lunch stop, and place to gather for all the latest news, this was the ideal place for me to hang out and try and find out about the drive that was due in.

Fort Worth was the favourite destination for hundreds of cowboys, buffalo hunters, railroad workers, and freighters eager to wash off the trail dust and enjoy themselves. The Store keep said it was a common sight for dozen or more of the festive cowboys, imbued with the spirit of pure devilishment, usually mounted on their horses, And is their custom to visit several dance houses, caroused and danced with the "girls," drink when they felt so disposed, and continued their career without much trouble until round about 1 o'clock, After mounting their horses, each drew his six-shooter, and blazing away in the air, firing many shots, at the same time putting spurs to their horses, they made tracks for the depot. The information the Store keep had told me was invaluable, the store was the ideal place to hang out to arrest the two outlaws the Judge intrusted me with. After a day exploring I made my way back to the Boarding house to rest, The landlady was very pleasant, and offered me some refreshments. I did not want to trust my luck and go to the Saloons, so I stayed in my room until the next day. Morning had arrived and it was time to meet up with the local Sheriff, I walked down to the courthouse Square where a tall well-dressed gentleman met me, not like any Sheriff I had come across before, Many of them were often rugged and dress like Cowhands, I suppose because we are in a large town they are more a custom to fine clothing and better conditions, I did think to myself this would suit me rather than being out on the trail for days on end.

He then handed me two wanted posters with a description of the two men and said the rest is up to you, I have two men as back up if you need them, I am sure you will handle it he said. It wasn't before long you could hear a loud noise of hooves, and a dust cloud followed, whistles and shouting, A large herd of longhorns coming through the street, many folks had moved on the boardwalks in fear of being trampled on, this was the drive coming into the depot, I looked upon the men riding but didn't recognise any of them that resembled the description, I followed on foot towards the depot and waited. The Cows were moved into pens at the depot then the dust started to clear many riders had dismounted and attended to their horses, then out of the corner of my eye I could see two more riders lacking behind, was this the men I thought to myself, As they got closer they were indeed the men that fitted the description, My mouth suddenly when dry again and my heart was racing, the adrenaline was kicking in, What's my next move I thought to myself?

I can't shoot then ask questions later, that would be no different to the outlaws and there would be mass gun fight with the other cowhands, I need a plan, I waited until the two men had attended to their horses and then followed them towards town. I could see both were carrying pistols in holsters and both had their saddlebags with them, My plan was to see were they went and who they met, The two men headed straight for the Saloon, just outside they turned as if they knew I was following them, they turned to each other started to talk then went in, I decided to back off and stood on the opposite side of the street, I checked my Pistol re holstered it and then decided to go in. It wasn't a large establishment but didn't have many people drinking and the smell of stale cigar smoke and stale beer was quite potent, the floor was covered in saw dust to soak up the mess, the men were sitting at a table with another man a well-dressed chap who didn't look like an outlaw, more of a businessman or of something of that line, I went to the bar and ordered a drink, I turned so I could keep watching them, As I took a sip on my drink, Then a drunk nudged me and said in a slurpy voice "buy me a drink stranger?" I looked at him them moved along the bar.

The three men was still talking, I thought this an ideal time to approach them I called to the Bar keep and said "another," As he was pouring my drink I quietly said to him to fetch the Sheriff, he obliged and went out back I presume out of the back door, I slowly walked over to the table, I don't even have to think about what I'm doing again, I pulled out the wanted posters and said hands on the table, both men looked up the third stood up and then moved away, on this I drew my pistol. As before, the weight is exactly right, the balance perfect. The cold steel of the barrel rests comfortably in my palm. I am so familiar with it that I don't even have to think about what I'm doing.

The sound is a release of power, a small explosion. I know how much energy is in the tiny cartridge, and how the energy is transformed when the cartridge hits the wall or ground. It's like a little lightning bolt going off, a tiny thunderstorm, and when you point the gun at someone, The sound reverberates through the room, and when it stops, everyone is quiet. Everyone is watching you. I didn't have to say a word. I don't need to explain anything. But this time I hit one man in the arm and the other the put his gun down, I clearly was too quick for the both of them, A few minutes passed which time seemed to stop, I named both men and held them there until the Sheriff arrived, The third man had seemed to of slipped away while all the commotion was going on, clearly a partner or a fence for stolen goods. The Sheriff and his two men came through the saloon door along with the bar keep, He said "good work Tate." They bound the two men, and I followed them to the Sheriff's office, The doctor met us at the office and patched up the man's arm as it was just a graze, then they were both locked up in Jail, The Sheriff gave me a coffee as he could see my adrenaline was still high. I sat on a chair in the Office, The Sheriff said that these two will be up before the Judge in the morning and he expects you to give your account of your arrest, I obliged and would see them in the morning, I felt quietly relieved that it was all over. The following morning I went over to the court house there was the Judge, The Sheriff his two deputies and myself, both men was brought forward to face the Judge, The Judge asked them both if they had anyone that was to represent them, one answered Mr Gibbs a lawyer from a small firm just the other side of town, not many people were in the court house at the time, The Judge proceeded with the prosecution of both men, the first man was named as Mr John W McNeil and the other Mr Robert H Greg both small time thieves and rustlers, charged with larceny from a ranch just outside Fort Worth and stealing two horses from the same ranch. Mr Gibbs gave their defence, then I was called to give my account of the arrest. Mr Gibbs questioned why I had shot at Mr John W McNeil, I explained my case and the Judge asked me to sit back down, After a short trial both men had been sentenced to 7 years imprisonment at the state penitentiary, The Sheriff met me outside the court house after the trial, and told me I have done a great job, and I was to take this note back to Marshal Chapman, when I leave for Whiteoak's. He said the Judge was pleased with me and would call again for my assistance, by this time I was hungry, before I left to go to the café, The Sheriff asked if I would stick around until my rent had finished, I obliged as it was a good opportunity to buy some new gear as mine had started to look tatty, and my pants were quite worn. I went off to the mercantile to buy new clothes. A few days had gone, and it was time to leave.

Chapter 7

13 Mile to Whiteoak's

The Marshal and a young deputy from Fort Worth "Tate" had been out through the plains and territories for nearly three weeks on the trail in search for a known bandit. He is known as 'Antonio' and described as a notorious badman and wanted for bank robbery, train robbery, cattle rustling and murder. He is about 6 foot 1 inches tall and has long silver hair, believed to be heavily armed and dangerous, and is a half breed Mexican. Marshal was well aware that he rode alongside two or three additional bandits. Could be more However, Despite the lack of information the identities of these elusive individuals remained concealed, shrouded in mystery.

The Marshal had ridden through the panhandle and onto the Indian territories where life can be very dangerous, mainly from Cherokee and the borders of Mexico the pair travelled hundreds of miles in search of these bandits. Life can indeed present itself as a perilous journey, particularly when one delves into the territories surrounding Cherokee and Comanche or ventures along the borders of Mexico. In these regions, the risks multiply, contributing to an environment where safety can feel like an elusive concept. Some individuals, with unwavering determination, brave the unknown, embarking on treacherous paths that span hundreds of miles in pursuit of these elusive bandits.

Rations was getting low, and both Marshal Chapman and his young Deputy Marshal Tate were very weary and still miles from Whiteoak's or even Fort Worth. The evening was drawing in and it was time for the Marshal to set up camp, for as nightfall approached, the Marshal made a calculated decision to establish their camp near a cluster of rocks in close proximity to a desiccated ravine. Acting with precision and expertise, they efficiently hitched their horses, ensuring their safety and comfort throughout the night. After removing the saddles, a subtle gesture of trust and bonding between the Marshal the two individuals made a calculated decision to ignite a modest fire. Fully aware of the inherent hostility of their surroundings, they understood the importance of maintaining vigilance. With one person dutifully assigned to keeping watch every couple of hours, they took proactive measures to ensure their safety, The Marshal was first to take watch. The coffee pot was on and there was plenty of jerky to replenish their hunger. It was a cloudy evening with no moonlight. The two swapped shifts, by this time Marshal was ready for some shuteye, The Marshal understood the importance of remaining vigilant and alert, aware that the perils of the night were yet to be vanquished. Despite his fatigue, he remained unwavering, displaying a commitment to his duty and the responsibility he held.

Morning broke and they both saddled up after their morning coffee, beans, and biscuits. Nothing was to report but a peaceful night. Frustration tinged their voices as they both decided it was time to regroup and head back south to Whiteoak's. With an air of professionalism, they acknowledged that sometimes even the most diligent efforts yield no immediate results. However, their resolve remained unwavering, knowing that their commitment to the trail would ultimately lead them closer to the truth. Whiteoak's was still four days' ride from their current position. The Marshal's wealth of experience as a seasoned old soldier made the trail nothing but familiar to him. Having faced countless journeys before, but on the other hand young Deputy Marshal Tate, despite his limited experience, approached his role with a commendable willingness to learn and grow under the guidance of the seasoned Marshal; After following a track, they came across a burnt-out wagon with debris strewn all over the track. The Marshall was a little suspicious of the circumstances. Tate said, "What happened to the wagon?" Marshal turned round to Tate and said, "It isn't Cherokees, looks like bandits to me," Tate replied, "How long ago was this wagon attacked, and where are the bodies?" Marshal replied, "Probably three weeks or more, either the owner escaped, or the predators have taken them." We should head on," Said the Marshal, As they rode on for another couple of hours, the anticipation of the unknown filled the air. The wind tousled their hair and the open road stretched out ahead, promising new discoveries. Suddenly, their eyes caught sight of a distant dust cloud, swirling and billowing in the distance. A mixture of excitement and caution stirred within the pair as they recognized the potential for unseen dangers lying ahead. The Marshal, with years of experience under his belt, couldn't help but be a little cautious and said it was either a herd of animals or more than 6 riders. He turned to Tate and said, "We will approach slowly." Both the Marshal and Tate rode on. By this time, they had caught up with the tracks this confirmed the Marshal's suspicions that it was around 8 horses. "Now that would be difficult for us!" said the Marshal, "If these were the Bandits, and they were actively searching for us, there's no doubt that we would be outgunned". With the adrenaline pumping and the survival instincts kicking in, they find themselves in an exhilarating, yet perilous situation. The Bandits are notorious for their firepower and lack of mercy. They are heavily armed and ruthless, leaving us with no choice but to rely on our wits and resourcefulness, The Marshal carried a Sharps rifle, a 44 Dragoon and a 36 pistol for close encounters, but on the other hand, Tate only had a 44/40 repeating rifle and a 36 pistol. They both headed towards higher ground to try and see if the Marshal could use his spyglass, by this time evening was drawing in again quickly.

Marshal said, "We will make camp by that rock, but no fire tonight so we don't attract any attention". Deputy Tate was a little jumpy as it was his second outing on a long hunt for outlaws.

Despite another day passing with no sight of the riders, the observant Marshal couldn't help but notice tracks leading back towards the town of Whiteoak's and then veering towards the New Mexico border. They had only a couple of days ride left before heading back into town. The Marshal was still cautious. As the protagonist he rode through the vast expanse, his keen eyes caught a glimpse of high ground in the distance. Determined to gain a better vantage point, he deftly ascended the terrain and reached for his spyglass. With the instrument clutched firmly in his hand, he peered through its lenses, patiently scanning the horizon. Moments passed, yet his perseverance paid off as the figures of riders materialized before him. It was a reward for his astute observation, a triumph of his unwavering focus and confirmed they were the bandits with a couple of loose horses, possibly from the wagon they saw earlier. In total 6 bandits, so the Marshal was right by saying there were possibly 8 horses.

By this time, they were approximately 2 days ride from Whiteoak's. The Marshal said to Tate "There's a small ravine just past that group of rocks called Dead Man's Finger," he stated resolutely. It was evident that he had meticulously planned their route. "We'll camp there tonight, strategically positioning ourselves to trap these outlaws in case they attack." His words held the weight of authority, leaving no room for doubt. The Marshal's unwavering commitment to his duty was felt in every syllable he spoke, fuelling the resolve of those under his command. Tate agreed, so they both dismounted to lead their horses by reign, so not much dust rose on the trail. They both found a spot in Dead Man's Finger and set up camp again. The Marshal said, "No fire again as we don't want to give our position away, Tate you take first watch." Two hours passed and the Marshal took over his watch, Tate was quick to get his head down and was soon asleep, The Marshal took a swig from his canteen then heard a rustle. The night was clear but no moon again. You could make out silhouettes and formations in the dark. Marshal picked up his rifle and took guard. From out of the darkness a figure appeared, then another. He knew straight away this was the Bandits. Clearly, they had doubled back. Marshal shouted out to Tate, 'Hey Kid, wake up!' He saw a flash, then heard the shot. A bullet had whizzed past and hit the rock behind. By this time, Tate had got his repeater and took a shot back.

The Marshal took cover near a large rock and the same for Tate. Six silhouettes in the dark could be seen by this time and started to fire. The Marshal called out "This is the US Marshal, put your weapons down and come in peacefully", The lead silhouette shouted back "My name is Antonio and by the time dawn will break you will be food for the buzzards". Again, a volley of fire got closer. The Marshal called at Tate and said, "Hold your ground!" But it was dark and difficult to see, he took a shot and hit one the of silhouettes. They hit the ground. By this time, they started to spread out. By now the odds were a little more even, again the Marshal called to Tate "Watch the rock behind you!" then another volley of fire came across again and became intense. Both Tate and the Marshal were pinned down in a night fire fight. Tate fired back with his repeater but from behind came a silhouette firing at Tate, he was hit, Marshal called out again to see how bad Tate was, "I've took a bullet to the leg," but the bandit had gone down too with the return fire. Then another Bandit came out the shrub and unleased the horses and fired before the horses fled. Marshal managed to hit him too. Suddenly there was quietness and the odour of spent powder as the smoke cleared through the darkness, Tate was slumped on the ground and bleeding out from his leg, but the fight seemed to be over. The Marshal went over to Tate, put a belt on his leg, pulled it tight and said, "Hold in there kid, we need to get you back to Whiteoak's."

Dawn had risen and the Marshal could see the extent on what happened. Three Bandits had been killed but Tate was wounded, and he needed to see a Doc as soon as possible. The horses had gone, but no sign of the Bandit tracks. There was too many tracks in the ground to even think about following if they found their horses.

The Marshall took a day's provisions from his saddle and said, "We've got to move back towards Whiteoak's before they come back." Tate managed to stand with the aid of a stick the Marshal found, and they both started to walk out of Dead Man's Finger. "It's about 13 miles to Whiteoak's." Said the Marshal. After several hours walking and short of water, a rider came into sight. The Marshal recognised the shape of the figure. It was Ranger Poncho. Him and

Soapy had heard the gunfire a couple of miles away and Poncho came out to investigate. The Marshal was relieved to see him and said, "You're a sight for sore eyes and that's a whiskey I owe you later." He then asked Poncho to take Deputy Tate back to Whiteoak's, and I'll track down our horses. The Ranger left with Tate, and the Marshal managed to catch up with both horses and headed back to Whiteoak's to file his report. Tate received immediate medical attention from the skilled hands of the Doc. The timely intervention ensured that his injuries were promptly patched up, providing a glimmer of hope for Tate's future rides. Although the prognosis was positive, it was essential for him to prioritize rest and recuperation to allow his body the time it needed to heal completely. Rest serves as an integral component in his journey back to the saddle, fostering a strong foundation for a successful return. With this professional guidance in mind, Tate can embrace this period of respite, For this young man he healed quickly, and Tate was soon ready to ride back out.

Chapter 8

A Map Maker's Tale:

Whiteoak's is a small frontier town consisting of 24 buildings and two streets, its inhabitants consist of 43 residences, and the rest is made up from miner's camps and passers through, many only stop for a few days as they travel through, they range from street sellers to ranch hands looking for work, but then it also attracts the lower kind, such as Street Urchins, Vagrants, Outlaw's, and Opportunists. Whiteoak's is a strategically positioned town, benefiting from its proximity to a spring that guarantees a constant supply of fresh water to its residents. However, this advantage comes at a price, as the town is located a two to three-day ride away from the nearest river. The terrain surrounding Whiteoak's is characterized by a captivating blend of desert rocks, deep ravines, and plentiful Texan trees and bushes. Such geographical features add a certain charm and uniqueness to the area. Situated in the Territories, Whiteoak's is conveniently positioned not far from the main trail to Mexico. Remarkably, the trail eventually forks towards New Mexico and the Panhandle, granting travellers bound for these destinations an advantageous starting point. This intriguing combination of natural and navigational features makes Whiteoak's a focal point for both residents and those passing through the area.. With over a week's ride to Fort Worth. It's a quite hostile place and not for the weak hearted. The discovery of Silver near the town saw the town grow from just a hand full of settlers to where it is now, bringing wealth and opportunities.

As the mist gently dissipates in the early morning, the once-fresh scent of nature transforms into something altogether more pungent. The air becomes thick with the unmistakable odour of putrid horse and cattle manure, intermingled with a hint of rotting food, as the sun rises higher in the sky. With the departure of the rains, the landscape begins its slow process of drying out, and the once-muddy grounds gradually give way to a dusty terrain. Even though the aroma may not be the most pleasant, this transformation serves as a reminder that nature is constantly in flux, adapting and evolving with each passing day, with the tracks in the main street from the wagons and riders, the streets are hardening from being a muddy deluge.

For most of the occupants, they are attending to their daily chores and the mercantile store is readying to open for just a normal day, The Saloon is being cleaned from the night before, Ms Dolly is close to ringing the School bell for the young children to attend School once they have done their daily duties. For many, they are doing their daily chores, they are chopping wood and collecting fresh water from the well, collecting eggs, milking the cows and other. The Sheriff is up and about, greeting the Marshal as he strolled through the bustling streets of the ordinary frontier town, coffee cup in hand, an adventurous energy filled the crisp morning air. The lively atmosphere was teeming with a sense of camaraderie as people greeted each other, their smiles betraying the shared experiences that had forged their tight-knit community. It was a sight to behold as normal life carried on, undeterred by the challenges that the frontier could bring. In the Marshal's eyes, this was not just a routine round, but an opportunity to venture into a world where every corner held a story waiting to be unravelled. With every step, the scent of freshly brewed coffee fuelled his spirit for exploration, infusing him with a daring resolve to protect and serve the town he held dear.

One of its occupants is Jeb, a young adventurer and amateur cartographer, the son of an Anglo German army officer who fought in the Franco-Prussian War, Jeb was accepted by the National Geographic on an exhibition to help map parts of South America particularly Peru and its coastline. He was looking for a passage back to England then onto Europe. While waiting in New York for his advancement from the National Geographic he was invited by another young fellow cartographer in New Hampshire, Wishing to map out parts of the Northwest Territories. Having already returned from a dangerous perilous environment he declined, just by chance he met Olive, both having English connections and education the pair decided to move south, and found haven in the frontier Town of Whiteoak's, setting up a small and prosperous Apothecary. Jeb worked for the Southern Railroad Surveying, but its completion was near.

On this particular day, he was about to start a new adventure by mapping out Stenson County and its borders for the governor of Whiteoak's as his employer. On its own could be a perilous job, this was an adventure by itself, due to its geographical position the likely hood of being highjacked, bushwacked or just murdered by outlaw's and opportunists and that's without the threat of Indians. Jeb an amateur cartographer had the chance to literally put Whiteoak's on the Map!

The Marshal suggested that he took a companion with him one that could shoot, but choosing the right one was difficult, Sheriff Smiff was tied up with normal town duties, the Marshal was already on Federal business and couldn't help, the Rangers were already out on the trail tracking down the remainder of the bandits who ambushed the Marshal and young deputy Marshall Tate earlier. There were no other candidates as many had other commitments, the choice was hard, but he finally persuaded someone to ride with him. With the provisions on a pack horse and Jeb waiting outside the Apothecary. his chosen companion finally rode up, Franco the Barber, he was originally from Italy and travelled to the states and had experience in the Army. "Morning," called Franco to Jeb. He replied, "are you ready sir?" then Franco replied, "sure am."

Jeb skilfully mounted his horse, exhibiting an air of confidence as he prepared to embark on their journey. With determination in his eyes, he and his trusty steed rode out, fully aware of the task that lay ahead. Their first objective was to travel to the border, enabling them to conduct a thorough survey of the area. However, Jeb couldn't help but notice that the supplies and equipment he had packed on the back of his horse seemed somewhat unwieldy. Understanding the unpredictable nature of their mission, Jeb and Franco were unsure of the exact duration it would take to accomplish their goal. Nevertheless, this minor inconvenience did not deter their commitment to the task at hand.

Following several days of travel, the weary pair finally arrived at the river. However, their path forward was obstructed by the formidable sight before them. The recent rainstorms had caused the river to swell, transforming it into a perilous force of nature. Realizing the inherent danger, Franco turned to his companion, Jeb, and uttered a grim warning. "We cannot attempt to cross here," he gravely remarked. His words conveyed both caution and professionalism, a clear acknowledgment of the potential hazards that lay ahead. The situation called for decisive and informed action, emphasizing the importance of prioritizing safety above all else. Jeb's agreement, the realization dawned upon the pair that they would need to find a suitable spot to cross, with no clear spot they found a group of rocks not far from the river's edge, Franco said that they will make camp there for tonight and hope the river recedes by morning.

The pair unsaddled their horses and made camp, lit a small fire and fresh coffee, Franco said did you hear that? It seemed to be hissing and rustling, Jeb said I'll check it out, he wandered down to near the bank of the river and saw there were lots of diamondback snakes moving along the riverbank, Before Jeb could turn back, a snake came out of nowhere and struck at Jeb, luckily he managed to move quickly and the snake missed his leg by a whisker, Jeb ran back and said we can't stop here it's infested with snakes. The recent storms had brought all the Snakes out. The pair packed up camp and moved inland a little but being very cautious, they found a more suitable spot this was difficult as it was near dusk. The pair finally settled down, As morning broke, they decided to find another crossing for the river, after an hour's ride, they finally found a place to cross, and the river had receded slightly, their horses weren't spooked, so they proceeded to cross. Jeb could finally start surveying the boarder, Jeb found an area, Franco held the measuring stick and Jeb started surveying and mapping out the contours. After several hours Jeb said to Franco "It's time to move on and map out the next section." Franco said, "this is going to take an age," Jeb reassured Franco and said, "luckily for us Stenson is a small county."

As the days had passed, the time had come for them to embark on the treacherous journey towards the Territories. Both of them were well aware that this leg of their expedition would be one of the most perilous, fraught with countless dangers in every turn in the untamed wilderness, one couldn't dismiss the fact that countless dangers lurked at every turn. Just weeks prior, a shocking incident unfolded when a wagon and its owner fell victim to a merciless Indian attack. This heart-wrenching event served as a stark reminder of the risks faced by those venturing off the beaten path.

Soon the pair reached their destination and wasted no time in setting up their equipment to begin the task at hand. They meticulously surveyed the area, every detail dissected and analysed with precision. However, as they focused on their work, a distant sight caught their attention, As Franco and Jeb stood side by side, their eyes collectively fixed on the distant horizon, a cloud of dust began to surge into the sky. Their gazes locked on the ominous sight, Franco couldn't suppress his mounting unease to Jeb and voiced his discontent, "I must admit, Jeb, the sight of that looming cloud of dust on the horizon does not bring me joy." His words, carefully chosen, hinted at deep-seated concern, reflecting the seriousness of the situation at hand. Jeb agreed, the pair packed their equipment and rode off to find somewhere safe, The pair found a ravine to stay safe until whatever it was, had passed. As the cloud drew nearer, gradually revealing its true nature, it became apparent to the observers that it was, in fact, a herd of cattle being guided by a group of experienced cowhands. The pair watched in awe as the animals gracefully moved across the horizon, their hooves gently thudding against the earth. The scene exuded a sense of mastery, with each cowhand skilfully orchestrating the movement of the herd, ensuring the safety and wellbeing of the animals under their care. As the tense atmosphere began to settle, a lone figure on horseback emerged from the horizon. Racing towards them, the rider's urgent cry echoed through the air, "Are you both alright?" They could sense the concern in their voice, each syllable imbued with a genuine worry. Not wasting a moment, the cowhand quickly informed them of the perilous discovery they had made a few miles behind. "We've seen signs of Indians," Jeb looked over at Franco as they were cautioned, their tone now filled with a sombre seriousness.

Each word carefully chosen to convey the importance of the message, reminding them of the looming danger that lay ahead. He wasn't sure that they were following them, but he also said too small for a war party, The cowhand was taking the herd to Fort Worth. Jeb agreed with Franco to ride out behind the drive as cover and resupply at Fort Worth. This growing city, saw Great Herds of Longhorns that were driven to the railheads in Kansas and Fort Worth was on the main route to the Chisholm Trail. Lowing herds camped near the town, and cowboys galloped into Fort Worth, firing their pistols into the air, and even riding their horses into the Saloons. The red-light district was one of the most infamous places in the area known as "Hell's Half Acre." Stagecoaches carried passengers and mail to points beyond. One line operated between Fort Worth and Fort Concho (San Angelo). A contract was let by the Post Office Department for a line between Fort Worth and Fort Yuma, Arizona, the longest daily stagecoach line in the world-approximately 1,500 miles. Plus, the railroad had several lines into the city. Not the ideal place to resupply but necessary, Jeb found a general store to purchase the goods they needed, but seeing what was on offer Franco headed straight for the Saloon, Jeb caught up with Franco after he brought the supplies and said, "we haven't got time for this," Franco agreed "but one more for the road." Just as they were about to leave the saloon, the cowhand that they saw a day earlier approached them, greeted them, and offered to buy them a whisky, they both agreed knowing this would be a bad idea. "Barkeep whiskies all round," Shouted the Cowhand as he had just been paid for bringing in the herd, by this time it was late afternoon and the three of them were slowly getting drunk, a poker player stood up from the table then said, "we don't like immigrants in here," Franco backed away and replied "Sporco porco chiamami ancora così, ti riempirò di piombo! His next breath was "we don't want any trouble," That was it, the poker player went to draw his pistol on Franco, but before Franco could draw his, the Cowhand stepped in and said, "that's enough gents, that's enough", For Jeb and Franco it was time to leave quickly, lucky for them, the Cowhand was known in Fort Worth, and he calmed down the poker player. They rode out quite hard until they reached the point that the horses were so tired, they couldn't ride anymore, "Phew that was a close call, we need to camp." said Jeb, Franco agreed the pair found an ideal spot near a rock and some Mesquite trees. Nobody had followed them out, they settled down by a campfire and had beans and salt pork for their supper.

The next morning, they left a bit later than normal just to give a little more time for the horses to recover from the hard ride out of Fort Worth. They finally got back to surveying the area when Franco stumbled on some old wooden boxes still sealed and had not been opened, the boxes lay behind a bushy area, intrigued he gradually opened one of the boxes only to find it empty. Unsure what he would find he was hoping for old treasure or something like that, but the contents, whatever it was had perished, He knew then this trip wasn't such a good idea after all and the pair were riding their luck, Jeb called to him and said I need you over here, Franco obliged.

After several hours surveying it was time to move on, they packed up the horses and continued, by this time they had reached another ravine, Franco and Jeb both agreed it was an ideal spot to set up camp for that night. Just as they were resting the horses and lighting the fire, they could hear other horses in the background, Franco said we must be on guard, Jeb not being good with a rifle or with a pistol, was quite nervous, But Franco came prepared with a 44/40 rifle and two colt 45's. It started to get dusk and the noise of the riders had gone, but suddenly from a distance Franco could see a small party of Indians heading their way. The pair wasn't sure how this would go, as a peace treaty was in place, but some renegade Indians attacked travellers, sheep herders and supply waggons, Franco could make out it was five or six riders, but it was too late to resaddle, and Jeb's equipment was too valuable to leave behind. For some reason the riders stayed back and just watched, Franco said "they're just watching," Jeb agreed, They maybe just after our supplies and horses, Franco said to "Jeb saddle up we try and make it back to Whiteoak's hopefully they should keep their distance," Franco stayed on guard while Jeb got the horses ready, It was intense as Jeb and Franco couldn't predict if they were going to attack.

With a sense of adventure coursing through their veins, the pair wasted no time in mounting their trusty horses and setting off at a brisk pace. The urgency in their movements indicated a desire to outrun any potential pursuers, and Franco, glancing over his shoulder, hoped to catch a glimpse of any signs of the elusive Indians. But to his surprise, they had vanished into thin air, leaving behind an air of mystery and a heightened sense of exhilaration for the daring duo. With their hearts pounding and adrenaline fuelling their ride, they pressed on. By this time morning had broken and the pair had been up all night. Franco said to Jeb "we'd better keep our wits about us," After several miles the pair slowed down to take a break and no riders were in the distance. "That was another close call," said Jeb, Franco agreed, Jeb also said, "We have three quarters of the surveying done we can head back and continue another time, I also must map out the town for the governor, if you're available once I've done that, we can finish Stenson County." Franco just nodded and tipped his hat as the pair headed back off, after a couple more day's ride, they arrived back at Whiteoak's. Olive greeted Jeb with open arms, and Franco took the horses back to be stabled. The governor sent the Town Mayor down to greet them and requested a report on the surveying. After a couple of hours with the Governor updating him and he was satisfied with what happened. Agreed to let them go back out to complete the Job, Jeb was quietly relieved that they still had their scalps.

A month had passed, and Jeb had finished mapping out the town, Franco and Jeb returned to their surveying duties with a determined mindset. It was time to go back out and complete the task of surveying the remaining parts of the county. Armed with their equipment and fortified with a sense of purpose, they methodically moved from one corner of the county to another, ensuring proper measurements and accurate documentation. Their professional tone was evident in their meticulous approach, maintaining a keen eye for detail and adhering to their rigorous standards. As they advanced through the remaining areas, Franco and Jeb encountered various challenges but not as before. Yet hoping that they didn't have a repeat of the breathtaking experiences from the last trip, and they would be safe and soon back in town.

Notes: Translation - Sporco porco, chiamami ancora così, ti riempirò di piombo!

"You dirty pig, call me that again, I'll fill you full of lead!"

Chapter 9

English Jack:

Known as English Jack, John was born in England from a wealthy Family highly educated after being schooled at a historic grammar school. Being from a wealthy family he did not have to work having an allowance each year. His family made their fortune from property and hotels in the height of the boom of industrialization, Like many other families with means, found their fortunes seeing the opportunity to increase their wealth by towns growing. This was the transition to new manufacturing processes in Britain and Continental Europe, and here in the States, which occurred during the period from around 1760 to about 1840. This transition included going from hand production methods to machines to new chemical manufacturing and iron production processes, the increasing use of waterpower and steam power, the development of machine tools, and the rise of the mechanized factory system. Output increased, and a result was an unprecedented rise in population and in the rate of population growth in towns and cities. The textile industry was the first to use modern production methods and textiles became the dominant industry in terms of employment, value of output, and capital invested.

The boom brought about an unprecedented increase in the wealth of Johns family, propelling them into a realm of extravagance. With riches at his disposal, John found himself grappling with a restlessness born out of not needing to work. The allure of leisure, once a distant dream, now left him craving for something more. His adventurous spirit yearned for excitement, urging him to forge a path that would keep him engaged and enthralled. As the opportunities beckoned, John set out on a quest to find the perfect endeavour that would occupy his time and satisfy his thirst for adventure. Little did he know that this path would lead him down an exhilarating journey, forever altering the course of his life and the legacy of his family.

The Voyage filled with a spirit of adventure and a desire for independence, John reached a pivotal moment in his life. After enduring countless arguments with his father, he felt an overwhelming urge to forge his own path. With a boldness that only the adventurous possess, he made a life-altering decision: to board a steam ship bound for the States, New York to be precise. In that moment, as he stood on the deck, he let the wind whip through his hair, symbolizing the freedom he craved from the constraints of his past. With a mixture of nerves and excitement, John embarked on a journey into the unknown, ready to prove himself and discover what destiny awaited him in the bustling streets of New York. Embarking on the voyage across the vast ocean was no small feat for intrepid explorers of yore. The passage, fraught with challenges, stretched across a seemingly endless six to eight weeks aboard a sail-powered vessel. These daring individuals braved treacherous winds and unpredictable seas, their spirits unyielding in the face of adversity. But, for those seeking a swifter and somewhat less arduous sojourn, the advent of steamships offered a glimmer of hope. Aboard the magnificent vessels propelled by the miraculous power of steam, the journey could be shortened to a mere two to four weeks, depending on the whims of the weather gods.

Little did he know that he would be spending the next few weeks in the not-so-glamorous Staten Island Quarantine. As he stepped foot into this makeshift haven with hundreds of eager immigrants, he couldn't help but feel a mix of excitement and trepidation. The conditions were far from ideal, with the cramped buildings and less-than-sanitary surroundings fuelling a sense of unease. However, he couldn't let this dampen his adventurous spirit. He understood that this was just a small hurdle on his quest to enter the country and pursue his dreams. With determination in his eyes, he vowed to remain resilient, making the most of this unexpected detour before finally embarking on the journey that lay ahead. John wasn't accustomed to this after being so wealthy, the terminals were busy people fighting to get their possessions. This caused John to move out quickly, but New York had become a slum and dangerous place to be as he soon learnt. As soon as John could leave New York, he brought a second-hand pistol, this was a colt, he already knew how to shoot, as being brought up with wealth, hunting was quite common, finding a good horse was another story, but he found one, as he wired for money to be sent over from England so he could continue on his journey. As John found solace in stopping in luxury rooms in hotels he travelled through Philadelphia Baltimore then on to the Capitol Washington Stopping in a luxury hotel, called 'The Willard,' John's first victim, This man came soon after he left New York, a lawless ruffian known as Bogue tried to hustle John in a game of poker, in a nearby Saloon one evening, Bogue was quite drunk, and John had his wits about him after leaving New York.

John got up from the card table after he had been insulted, John was very patriotic towards his Queen and country, Bogue had used this for the insult, Bogue turned to John and pulled his Colt Walker, A large but deadly gun at John, but his Walker missed fired and shot himself in the foot, miss firing was a common fault with the walker. John then saw the opportunity to draw his colt and took a shot at Bogue killing him instantly, after all the smoke had cleared the local Sheriff was called for, John knew he had to flee.

He quickly left to the hotel to collect his possibles and horse, then came victim number two, an eyewitness had followed him to the Willard and waited out of sight until John came out to fetch his horse. Chas Wittington the eyewitness thought he could cash in with the Sheriff and collar him, John just about to mount his horse Chas Wittington jumped out from a nearby bush spooking the horse, the horse reared up and, on the way, down struck Chas Wittington, he later died from a head injury. John mounted and then rode towards

Virginia on to Richmond where he could catch a train south. By this time the Sheriff had issued a warrant for his arrest, one witness said he thought his name was Jack and he was from England, So English Jack was born, As John remembered the day he'd stepped off the boat, for a fresh start in a new land, filled with hope and determination. But fate had a cruel sense of humour, and it had landed him right in the middle of this mess.

Victim number three came after John headed towards Texas Near Nashville Tennessee, He stopped to wire for money to be sent across, but after being declined from the bank he wasn't sure whether his father had done this just to spite him, John was desperate for money to feed his luxury. He found a small mercantile store, he masked up entered the store with his colt and robbed the store from cash, John found this thrilling as the danger that comes with robbery. John ran out of the store followed by the storekeeper shouting, "thief! fetch the Sheriff" John quickly mounted his horse turned and fired warning shots at the store keep, but fatally hitting the keeper. Finding robbery easy John soon robbed many more Mercantile stores for a quick dollar.

Heading towards Mississippi, came victim number four, holding up a stage with only two passengers he took his English charm as the two passengers were two ladies heading towards New Orleans this would later come back to bite John. This so-called easy picking with the stage he later held up another one that came along this route but his time the driver had company with a shotgun, a man called Wil Chaplin riding shotgun saw John and took a warning shot at him but being quick on the draw John hit Wil Chaplin fatally and then the stage stopped, again easy pickings robbing the occupants who had plenty of cash. Unknown to John he was leaving bodies and soon became someone of interest to the Marshals soon issued a warrant.

John eagerly embarked on a journey towards New Orleans in search of the vibrant blend of culture and music that echoes through the city's veins. As he meandered through the mesmerizing streets of the French Quarter, John's wanderlust led him to the Omni Royal

Orleans—a true gem among the city's oldest hotels. With its rich history and charming elegance, the Omni Royal Orleans offered a perfect sanctuary for John's immersion in the heart and soul of New Orleans. From the moment he stepped foot inside, he could almost feel the echoes of melodies mingling with whispers of captivating stories. It was as if the very walls of the hotel held the secrets of countless musicians and cultural icons who had passed through its doors. Liking the high life had to come to an end with victim number five.

Whilst playing poker near the old Pirate's Alley in an Saloon he was recognized by a young lady and her French companion, unknown to John this was one of the ladies that he robbed on a Stage heading towards New Orleans, Her French companion Théo Deschamps drew his pistol but was too slow, John shot dead Deschamps before he unholstered his pistol, With the commotion a fight broke out, John headed back to Omni Royal Orleans knowing that he had to leave quickly. He soon realised that he was running out of places to go, being wanted was difficult and going off the original trails to prevent getting caught by the law. John headed towards Houston, he's next two victims were two bounty hunter's that had tracked him down to the outskirts of Houston, John found a trading post to refresh his horse, while taking refreshments the two bounty hunters entered the wooden shack, John was at a table eating, the two men confronted him, John replied, "are you here for me?" one of the men said "yep we are going to take you in up to you on how?" They asked him to loosen his pistol belt and hand it over, John did this slowly, but they didn't take into account that John had a small 31 in his pocket as they took the belt, John asked, "do you mind if I had a smoke?" they both said "No, but reach for your pocket slowly," as John reached for his pocket, he drew the 31 and killed both men. Victim number 8 was the trading post keeper as he was a witness to the two men's deaths. By this time John found it too easy to get away with his crimes and he decided to up the ante. He began to kill more people, not just so he could get away, but for the thrill of it. John mounted his horse and headed into Houston knowing that it won't be long before those bodies would be found.

He headed towards a town called Laredo where he found a nice hotel and to stay low for a while, 200 miles or so was Whiteoak Springs, here he also found a room to stay in the governors building as being a frontier town wires often didn't reach the Marshal or Sherriff, they had to rely on the Stage or to travel too Forth Worth to collect federal papers etc. John finally found somewhere to hide in plain sight until victim number nine.

The Whiteoak Gazette reported this as - One eyewitness said, "this was cold blooded murder a man gunned down in the main street of Whiteoak's," The victim's name had not yet been released but suspected to be a Cowhand from Stenson Ranch, his assailant believed to be 'English Jack' he was recognized drinking whisky in the Saloon, English Jack came out and accused the cowhand of insulting him publicly, in which the cowhand denied. Unknown to John the cowhand was unarmed, he reached for his inside pocket for his tobacco tin, John mistaken the tin for a pocket pistol, John drew his colt and shot the cowhand dead and left him in the Street, reportedly going back into the Saloon to finish his whisky, The Marshal and Sheriff Smiff was called for, by the time they approached the scene John had already rode off, Number nine now to add to this gunman's tally and widely feared in the County, I suspect that the Marshal will have his work cut out tracking down this killer.

The Marshal published a warrant for him last April his description was as follows 'An Educated Gentleman going by the name of 'English Jack' Self Acclaimed Gunslinger and has claimed to have killed 8 men, Also Robbed General stores, banks, and Stagecoaches. Very well dressed approx. 5'11 inches tall, short brown hair, do not approach as extremely armed and dangerous Normally carries a 45 Colt with an Ivory handle. and a 31, Last seen near Stenson County. He added do not approach this man as he is extremely dangerous, John is known to travel from town to town using hotel rooms as residence and gambling in the nearest Saloon also to be flirtatious with the young ladies. 'JOHN WANTED DEAD OR ALIVE'

John rode off to find a safe place to stop until the heat had cooled down. In the high-stakes game of survival that John found himself in, the stakes were undeniably sky-high. As he galloped away, he couldn't help but feel a sense of relief wash over him. But this feeling was short-lived, as he knew that the danger was far from over. He had to find a place to lay low and figure out his next move. Branded with the ominous label of "Wanted Dead or Alive," he understood the gravity of the situation. With steely determination his instincts guiding him towards a safe haven. John knew that finding respite was imperative, a sanctuary where he could lay low until the heat had cooled down. In this dangerous game of cat and mouse, his professional manner he remained intact even in the face of adversity. With each gallop, he remained focused and calculated, determined to outrun the consequences that threatened to swallow him whole. John found another small town to lay low until he could figure out his next move. He arrived at the town just as the sun was setting, casting an orange glow over the dilapidated buildings and dusty streets. The air smelled of wood smoke and sagebrush. He found a cheap room above a Saloon and settled in for the night. As he lay on his hard mattress, he couldn't help but feel a sense of foreboding. Tomorrow, he would have to find a job, blend in, and hope that no one recognized him.

Chapter 10

Ms Kitty's Downfall: (The house of Ill repute)

Ms. Kitty's establishment is a shining example of a clean and licensed place where no expense is spared to ensure the utmost comfort and well-being of its clientele. From the moment you step through the doors, you are enveloped in an atmosphere of elegance and refinement, with every corner exuding a sense of timeless charm. The working girls, carefully chosen and impeccably cared for, are no exception with the girls full of beauty and grace, these girls bring an enchanting ambiance to this esteemed establishment. Ms Kitty's girls, renowned for their impeccable elegance, were not solely confined to Ms. Kitty's establishment but also often found in the Painted Pony Saloon.

Ms. Kitty's commitment to professionalism is evident in every detail, ensuring an unforgettable experience for all who visit, but she was in the habit to like a drink or two. Mainly passers-through and cowhands make up the majority of individuals who visit this establishment it is worth noting, and that these visitors come from a variety of backgrounds and bring with them a sense of adventure and ruggedness. The cross-section of characters that frequent this place adds a unique dynamic to the atmosphere.

Marshal Chapman, being a responsible and diligent individual, took it upon himself to ensure that the girls were regularly inspected by Doc, With a professional demeanour and a commitment to their well-being, he understood the importance of maintaining their health, By organizing regular appointments and coordinating with the Doc, Ms. Kitty, renowned for her sharp instincts and relentless pursuit of making money found this an added bonus. People started to make comments about the Marshal saying he was taking a back hander for doing this, but he was just concerned for the welfare of the girls, he had seen enough girls fall by the wayside, and he saw firsthand how easily girls could be led astray or marginalized within society and witnessed numerous instances where young women had succumbed to various challenges and adversities through ill health from sexual diseases and often dying or even jailed for long terms. In the beginning Ms Kitty was a daughter of a boarding house owner in New York, of Scottish heritage, but with the constant trouble with gangs and rioting in the area, this was a rough part of town, Its prevailing conditions and circumstances posed unique challenges to all, derelict, run down properties and overcrowding, left many families to move on, Ms Kitty and her parents were forced to close down the boarding house and as Ms Kitty only being at a young age in her teens, she was schooled by her educated father, despite the bleak circumstances of living in poverty, Ms Kitty was determined to provide for her family.

She embarked on a brave endeavour and started working in local Saloons, by sweeping floors clearing spittoons and glasses, this an unsafe environment as it had many ruffians, Undeterred by the rough crowd, she not only navigated the turbulent waters of the Saloon she managed to make a little money in this unclean job, once older she moved on to more challenging work within the Saloon environment. It's almost like a rite of passage, isn't it? The older one gets, the more they yearn for something more, something that pushes the boundaries of their skills and tests their wit. The Saloon hold compelling narratives within the intoxicating world.

As the Orange Riots took place in Manhattan, New York City, in 1870 and 1871, and they involved violent conflict between Irish Protestants who were members of the Orange Order and hence called "Orangemen", and Irish Catholics, along with the New York City Police Department and the New York State National Guard. The riot caused the deaths of over 60 civilians - mostly Irish labourers - and three guardsmen. But innocent civilians were caught up in violence including Miss Kitty's parents, Miss Kitty, feeling a profound sense of uncertainty and vulnerability, made the difficult decision to let go of her current situation and embark on a new journey. With only a few dollars tucked away in her purse, she resolved to head South, exploring the unknown and relying on her resourcefulness. Despite feeling unsafe, she pressed forward, navigating life by working tirelessly, from one Saloon to another. This bold decision to embrace change showcases Miss Kitty's resilience and soon started to collect a few hundred dollars, On her travels she met Carlos, A cowhand a determined and spirited young man, embarked on a quest for adventure driving cattle. With a twinkle in his eye and an insatiable hunger for the unknown, they set off to travel the vast untamed landscapes in search of thrills that could only be found amongst the dust and wildness, from town to town they soon married, as time went on the couple arrived at Whiteoak's and Ms Kitty after enduring countless months of traveling, Ms. Kitty found herself growing increasingly weary. Having explored various destinations and encountered numerous experiences along the way, her fatigue was understandable. Seeking respite and the comfort of a stable home, it came as a relief to finally settle in at Whiteoak's. The arduousness of their travels had taken its toll, leaving Ms. Kitty yearning for a sense of stability and longing to put down roots in this new and promising chapter of their lives.

Ms Kitty finally opened a small boarding house, Ms. Kitty's ensured that it would poise to become a haven for weary travellers and those seeking a homely atmosphere away from home. This venture represents a significant milestone in Ms. Kitty's career, as she aimed to create a space that exudes professionalism and caters to the diverse needs of her guests. From a couple of cozy private rooms and a communal area designed for social interaction, every aspect of this small boarding house has been thoughtfully and meticulously crafted to ensure the utmost comfort and satisfaction. Ms. Kitty's unwavering commitment to providing impeccable service coupled with her attention to detail guarantees that each guest's stay will be an experience to remember. But her rooms and rent were too expensive for the clientele and Whiteoak's was a new and growing frontier town. many of its visitors were Cowhands, Vagrants and Miners all looking for work at Whiteoak's, with the exception of explorers eagerly searching for hidden treasures and thriving on the challenges that awaited them around every corner. In this untamed territory, they found freedom, pushing the boundaries of their own courage, and forging a connection with nature that could never be replicated. drawn to the untamed wilderness that stretched for miles around.

It wasn't long before Ms Kitty, a discerning businesswoman, astutely recognized an opportunity to transform the boarding establishment into a house of ill repute. Embracing a professional tone, she meticulously studied the market and devised a comprehensive plan to seamlessly transition the premises into a more lucrative enterprise. With meticulous attention to detail, Ms Kitty envisioned an enticing atmosphere that would cater to the desires of discerning clientele, Cowhands and passers-through this wasn't out its own trouble, The Whiteoak's Gazette, faithful to its commitment to uncovering local matters, consistently reported on these minor crimes however small or large. However, rather than succumbing to the negative publicity, Ms. Kitty chose to capitalize on the situation, rebranding the boarding house to create a unique and alluring atmosphere that would intrigue those curious about the hidden underbelly of society. But the local branch of Whiteoak's Temperance Society, these ladies were filled with an unwavering determination often gathered outside Miss Kitty's establishment to protest. It was evident that they meant business, their resolve shining through their stern expressions. Clad in their resolute demeanour, they stood united, ready to tackle the challenges that came their way. The air was thick with purpose as their tone of voice echoed through the streets, demanding change and reform. Miss Kitty's, known for its association with excess and indulgence, had become the symbol of a societal issue that they were determined to address head-on.

These ladies, armed with their unwavering dedication and an unyielding belief in their cause. One unfortunate situation unfolded one afternoon when Mr. Willis, a well-known resident in town, succumbed to the lure of excessive drinking. Regrettably, his vices led him astray, leaving behind his wife and children in a state of utter destitution. It was revealed that Mr. Willis had recklessly squandered an entire month's worth of wages on his habit at Ms Kittys and disregarding his familial responsibilities. Marshal Chapman repeatedly apprehend Mr Willis for his unlawful activities and behaviour, Chapman's ability to remain calm and composed during challenging situations outside of Ms Kittys. Ms. Kitty's husband, Carlos, had grown weary of the persistent stream of minor crimes and the unwanted attention that seemed to gravitate towards his beloved Ms. Kitty. Despite their best efforts, the mischievous antics of Ms. Kitty never failed to attract curious onlookers, creating a never-ending cycle of chaos and commotion. The constant deluge of girls coming in and out endless flow of cowhands and other clients, As he pondered a solution to this predicament, Carlos's steadfast determination to restore a sense of order to their lives, slowly their lives had begun to change and in hindsight, this union proved to be an unfortunate mistake.

Despite the initial attraction and shared experiences, they soon discovered fundamental differences that strained their relationship. Their varying values, aspirations, and approaches to life gradually revealed irreconcilable conflicts, leading to a growing sense of dissatisfaction. Though marriage is often romanticized, the reality was far from idyllic. This experience served as a poignant reminder that even the most promising encounters can sometimes lead to regrettable outcomes, In this instance, Carlos found himself facing such a sobering realization. Despite its initial allure, the connection that had formed with Ms. Kitty had unfortunately taken an unexpected turn. Carlos, perhaps reluctantly, made the difficult decision to part ways with Ms. Kitty, leaving her to navigate her own path. This sombre reminder serves as a valuable lesson, highlighting the unpredictable nature of human connections and the importance of carefully assessing the potential consequences before embarking on a new venture. Carlos left and embarked on a new venture, a trail boss,

Carlos would oversee the coordination of cattle drives and ensure the safe movement of livestock from one location to another, As he rode off into the distance, it became clear that this marked the end of Carlos's association with Ms. Kitty and Whiteoak's.

After a while, a significant number of girls had ventured into the town of Whiteoak's, this became an arousing concern for Marshal Chapman and Sheriff Smiff, especially due to their lack of proper licensing and cleanliness, Sheriff Smiff immediately undertook the responsibility of addressing these concerns by initiating an organized effort to ensure the licensing of every newcomer, striving to maintain order and legality within their jurisdiction but this was difficult. One particular occasion, some of the girls refused to be licensed, and it was a public offence to solicit outside of the boundaries of Whiteoak's. If these Girls didn't comply they found themselves in front of Judge Pee, and she ensures that justice is served, and that appropriate consequences are imposed for the non-compliant behaviour. Judge Pee can contribute to maintaining order and promoting the principles of justice within the legal system. One particular Girl made the Gazette twice, Madam Lucy Lee, a mixed race girl of oriental descent had been soliciting without a licence, and using unlawful behaviour while supplying Opiates, she had found herself for the first time in front of Judge Pee, Ms Lee was accused of prostitution without a license but was later acquitted due to lack of evidence, but shortly after, she was re-arrested by Sheriff Smiff, and was found guilty, She was ordered to pay a fine of $4 and to apply for a Licence after an inspection from the Doc, but later left the town without complying with Judge Pee's order.

Ms. Kitty cautiously observed the escalating unrest in the town, as her renowned establishment, and her working girls, thrived amidst of it all. It wasn't too long before a notorious character entered the town, a known ruffian by the name of Leone. Picture a figure with a mischievous glint in his eye, always causing some sort of commotion wherever he went, despite his rather dubious reputation, there was something oddly captivating about Leone. He had a way of carrying himself that exuded an air of nonchalance, as if he were simply strolling through life without a care in the world. With his slicked back hair and tattered clothing, he was a true embodiment of the phrase "relaxed, yet dangerous." While some feared his presence, others found themselves strangely drawn to his charismatic charm. He caught the eye of Ms Kitty, inexplicably captivated by his enigmatic charm. In an intriguing twist of fate, It seemed that his laid-back demeanour and effortless magnetism were the perfect match for her free-spirited nature. Despite the initial reservations held by some, there was an undeniable allure to his relaxed tone, drawing people into his orbit with an undeniable gravitational force. Unknown to Sheriff Smiff and the Marshal, Leone was not only a wanted fugitive in their jurisdiction but also in several other states for petty larceny and other offenses, he was known as 'Leone the blade'. His eyes were a piercing shade of blue that seemed to look right through you, his build was that of a man who had seen his fair share of fights and survived them all. His dark hair was always slicked back, and he had a scar running diagonally across his left cheek. Despite his intimidating appearance, This startling revelation he had managed to evade from Sheriff Smiff and Marshal Chapman. It has become evident that Ms Kitty and Leone encounters have intensified, leading to an increased frequency of their interactions. This growing connection between the two parties has not gone unnoticed, as their presence in each other's lives has become more pronounced. The recent developments in the relationship between Leone and Ms. Kitty have raised eyebrows among the townsfolk, as Leone seems to be making himself at home at Ms. Kitty's establishment.

This evolving dynamic had sparked a sense of horror and disapproval among some members of the community, who find it scandalous that Ms. Kitty was a married woman, and she would allow a man to reside with her. Alas due to the nature of her business the townsfolk soon forgot. Leone relentless opportunism knows no bounds, as he is already on the hunt for a chance to exploit the unsuspecting Ms Kitty.

With his cunning and calculated nature, Leone eyes light up at the mere possibility of capitalizing on her vulnerability. Like a clever fox sniffing out its prey, he scours every interaction for the slightest crack in her armour. Whether it is her kind heart, her trusting nature, or even her good intentions, Leone wasted no time in seizing upon any opportunity that presents itself. Without a doubt, it became strikingly evident that the downfall of Ms. Kitty's establishment was imminent. The signs were as clear as daylight, leaving no room for doubt or speculation. It was a culmination of factors, each more persuasive than the last, that led to this unfortunate conclusion. Leone had rode out for a few days, it was business as usual at Ms Kitty's, but little did Ms Kitty know Leone, the audacious rogue with a flair for intrigue, had just executed the daring heist of the century - robbing a train across the border in New Mexico. The train robbery that day would forever bind him and his men together, forming an unshakeable bond forged through the fires of danger. With hearts pounding and adrenaline coursing through their veins, they set their plan into motion, their eyes locked on the prize. As the train barrelled through the moonlit night, they executed their perfectly choreographed heist with a precision befitting of seasoned outlaws. It was a spectacle that defied the laws of normalcy and elevated them to legendary status.

When the dust settled and the authorities were left dumbfounded in their wake, they stood tall, each clutching their share of the hard-earned loot tightly in their hands. Their escapade, brimming with excitement and risk, would forever remain etched in the annals of audacious adventure. With finesse, he outwitted the most formidable security measures, leaving authorities dumbfounded and passengers in awe. This act of impudence, while illicit in nature, showcased Leone unrivalled prowess and audacity. The sensational nature of his crime begged the question: who could resist being enthralled by the audacious exploits of such a captivating rogue? As they all successfully escaped with their hard-earned shares of the loot, Leone determination ignited an adventurous spark within him. Though the journey had been treacherous and filled with obstacles, his mind was already set on heading back to Whiteoak's, where he knew he could hide his newfound wealth. With a glint in his eye and a mischievous smile, Leone eagerly plotted his course back, evading any lawmen envisioning the thrill of what awaited him. The prospect of embarking on yet another daring escapade, this time with his newfound fortune, filled his heart with adrenaline, he rode back into Whiteoak's, but news had travelled to Whiteoak's especially to Sheriff Smiff and the Marshal that a train had been robbed, Whiteoak's was buzzing with excitement as news of a daring train robbery spread like wildfire. It was a tale that captured the attention of every townsfolk, The whispers of this audacious heist vibrated through the atmosphere, igniting a sense of exhilaration. It was thought of a bandit gang outsmarting the iron horse, snatching away its precious cargo, that fuelled their adventurous spirits. But easily picking up the whispers of any newcomer who dared to enter their jurisdiction. any notorious gang had been wreaking havoc wouldn't go unnoticed, and these lawmen were determined to outsmart and outwit anyone suspected to be a part of the robbery.

As Leone came back into Whiteoak's he went straight into the Saloon a brought himself a Whisky, so far not being a suspect, One of Ms Kittys Girls had noticed him, With a sense of urgency and an understanding of the importance of her discovery, she swiftly left the hustle and bustle of the saloon to relay the news to Ms. Kitty herself. The persuasive tone in her voice was undeniable as she urged Ms. Kitty to promptly attend to the return of Leone. Knowing the power and influence Leone held, the urgency in her voice was a testament to the potential consequences that awaited. Ms. Kitty could not ignore the gravity of the situation, and with a determined stride, she made her way towards the saloon's entrance, ready to face whatever Leone had brought back with him from his ventures. She was unaware of the fact that Leone had just robbed the train. The sense of anticipation and resolve in their demeanour was unwavering, as they embraced at the Saloon bar.

Little did she know, the gravity of the situation he had put them in. As they went back to her place, Ms. Kitty, with raised eyebrows and a hint of suspicion in her voice, demanded to know where he had been all this time. All he could muster as a response was a feeble, stuttered explanation, just on Business however, his words were laced with a persuasive tone, as he desperately tried to convince her of his innocence. She knew he had been up to no good Yet, lurking beneath the surface, she could sense the shadowy truth that contradicted his honeyed promises. It was in the slight tremor of his voice, the evasive glances he cast away, and the uneasy clench of his fists. She knew deep down that he had been up to no good, despite his artful attempts to manipulate her perception. Though the persuasive script danced before her, enticing her to believe, her instincts anchored her to a reality where his deceit loomed large.

He then said we might have to leave for a while It was during this precarious moment that he spoke up, his voice filled with a sense of urgency and concern. Delicately, he unveiled the possibility of an unsettling reality, Ms Kitty looked in horror, and called to him "What have you done?" He then proceeded to paint a vivid picture of the looming dangers and the paramount importance of safeguarding themselves, the weight of his words resonated deeply, compelling us to consider the difficult decision at hand. But unknown to Leone and Ms Kitty, a crucial development had taken place at the Marshal's Office. A detailed description of the robber's had been received from one of the victims on the train. This information had the potential to unearth valuable leads to the ongoing investigation and to point the finger at Leone, while the unsuspecting duo continued their quest for answers from each other and as the tension grew, Leone made a shocking confession - he had been the one who robbed the train. Ms. Kitty, overwhelmed by disbelief, found herself at a loss for words. In that very moment, a sea of questions flooded her mind. How could someone she had entrusted her faith in turn out to be the culprit? What other secrets lay hidden beneath the surface of their seemingly harmonious journey? Despite the shockwaves that reverberated through their relationship, the quest for answers continued, forcing both Leone and Ms. Kitty to confront the complexities that lay in their pursuit of truth, ultimately unveiling more than they bargained for.

While Leone confessed he had robbed the train, and Ms Kitty was in disbelief, The Marshal a dedicated and meticulous man wasted no time in analysing the received description. Marshal Chapman headed off to Sheriff Smiff to inform him, this meant certain death or heavy imprisonment if Leone was caught. The stakes had been raised, and the mere thought of being captured sent a shiver of excitement down their spines. It was as if the universe had issued a direct challenge, daring them to outsmart Sheriff Smiff and Marshal Chapman. That evening, as the sun began its descent, a soft knock echoed through the halls of Mr. Thomas's house. It was none other than Ms. Kitty, known for her charming demeanour and pleasant smile. Mr. Thomas, a distinguished man who held the titles of both bank manager and owner, opened the door with a warm welcoming gesture. As they exchanged pleasantries, the conversation flowed effortlessly, filled with laughter Ms Kitty asked if she could make a withdrawal of her savings and then she added a touch of humour to her request, Mr. Thomas agreed to her peculiar request, although he couldn't help but find it a tad strange. Setting off for the bank together, Mr. Thomas couldn't shake off his concerns about her actions. The money was placed into a large holdall bag and Ms Kitty stealthily bid Mr Thomas a good night, she vanished into the enveloping darkness. However, the following day, the tranquillity was shattered as Sheriff Smiff and Marshall Chapman pounded on Ms Kitty's door, eager to carry out their duties to find Leone. To their surprise and disbelief, the door swung open effortlessly, revealing an empty house devoid of any inhabitants. The absence of Ms Kitty left the pair perplexed, then the penny dropped, Marshal Chapman and Sheriff Smiff knew that she was involved somehow, As they were standing there Mr Thomas was walking to the Bank to open up as he did every morning, He politely said "Good morning gentlemen," Sheriff Smiff replied in an unsavoury manor then asked Mr Thomas if he had seen Ms Kitty,

"Yes," he replied, she came to me last night to request to withdraw her savings, I did think it a little odd but nevertheless she had a charm over me. Leone and Ms Kitty had vanished. Marshal Chapman and Sheriff Smiff finally issued two wanted posters Ms Kitty was wanted for harbouring known ruffians, had having a connection to a train Robbery and Embezzlement, While Leone robbing the train in New Mexico, he is known as a meanness and ruffian.

In the circumstances, Mr. Thomas had no choice to foreclosure on Ms. Kitty's property, it was essential to approach the matter, as Ms. Kitty and Leone are now wanted outlaws. Mr Dodger, a distinguished undertaker known for his astute business acumen, swiftly seized the opportunity presented by the availability of the property. With a shrewd eye for investment, he recognized the potential of the location and wasted no time in making his move. Mr Dodger's reputation as a professional in the mortuary industry preceded him and Ms Kitty changed to the undertakers.

This chapter doesn't end here, Whiteoak's welcomed two new members to its fold, Mose and Madam Lil, Who have taken over the old Doc's building, Work will commence after January for a new House of ill repute, The Gazette understands that it will be taking over from Miss Kittys old establishment. This will be a relief for those working girls that was left to work the Saloon, At least they will have their own grand building and will be properly looked after again to the relief to Sheriff Smiff and the Marshal, It's not without controversy though, Mose is Whiteoak's first man of colour, a free man from Lincoln's Emancipation, he also was a former Buffalo Soldier he had served in 10th the Cavalry Regiment, a man to be feared on the frontier.

Chapter 11

A New Day:

As the new day rises, as the sun comes up its a bright morning, Wells Fargo have announced that the stagecoach would be arriving later in the day, a normal day but for some residents a surprise maybe on the stage, Ms Maria Montez an actress and dancer. She achieved popularity throughout Europe, dancer, but the rumours told that she was a mistress of the King of Bavaria. Ms Maria Montez fled due to the German revolutions and found herself in London, she started with a promising dance career before men in the audience recognized her from the local newspapers and she was forced to flee back to the continent, Travelling her way around Europe, and there she established herself as an actress, singer, and dancer, Finally fleeing to America.

She had become admired by many gentlemen. Unknown to the Sheriff that she was on the stagecoach, plus nobody had greeted her or to show her to her room, She was only stopping for a few days until the next coach to Fort Worth arrives, where she is to play the theatre. As she stepped off the Stagecoach, Whiteoak's was the most Idyllic place she had seen for a while, The town was full of life and energy, with its bustling main Street. Marshal Chapman instantly recognised the young lady from advertisements in Fort Worth and walked down to greet her, Sheriff Smiff watched in disbelief, as it looked like Marshal Chapman was about to woo the young lady and he was twice her age and old enough to be her father, On the contrary Marshal Chapman only showed her common courtesy and escorted her to her lodgings, a room at the Governors Building where she rented one of the rooms.

Young Tate had gone back to Fort Worth, and he wasn't due back until the end of the month which left his room vacant. As the

Marshal walked away, Sheriff Smiff ran over to the Marshal to ask who the young lady was, The Sheriff was acting like a young puppy and very ungentlemanly as if he'd had never seen a woman before, The Marshal explained to Sheriff Smiff that she was a young actress and dancer, but wasn't due to star in our Saloon but in Fort Worth, The Sheriff was quite smitten at this point much to the annoyance to his wife Shelly. News had soon travelled through the town that we had somewhat of a well-known star in our mists, Many had not of herd of Ms Maria Montez but with her long dark hair soft eyes and very fair complexion. Many were waiting to get a glimpse of the young lady, outside the Governors building, Sherriff Smiff kindly went over to disperse the crowd of people that had gathered, But Ms Maria Montez obliged the crowd and said a few kind words, the crowd soon dispersed with an air of excitement.

Whiteoak's consists of mostly Married Gentlemen, only a few young suitors but the likes of Ms Maria Montez wouldn't entertain the likes of miners, cowhands but possibly a single Gentleman such as JP.

Later that day, A knock on the door of the Marshals Office "Come in" Said the Marshal, Then the door creaked open, Ms Maria Montez who stepped inside the room, she was a vision of loveliness and beauty. I had met a few wealthy people in my life, but never someone as richly dressed as her. Her dark brown hair was pulled up on her head into a beautiful hairstyle. A large white bow sat on top, and she wore a dress made of blue silk with delicate, hand-stitched flowers decorating the sleeves and hem of the skirt. It was the height of fashion, and even I knew this dress cost a lot of money.

She was tall and willowy and held herself straight and tall as she walked across the room, I asked, "can I help you?" she replied, "Yes would you escort me to the Saloon," but with a smile that would have won any heart of a man in a moment, I replied, "Yes." Knowingly to introduce to her to some of the dignitaries of the town, Marshal had wisely known that the Governor the Town Mayor and others of commerce would be in there.

As Ms. Montez and the Marshal stepped out of his office, A young man who appeared to be waiting outside for her, was a handsome well-built and dressed fellow. I knew that he was a man who worked at the bank part time. He turned to Ms. Montez and said, "may I come with you" in a nervous quiet voice, "of cause," as we walked down from the Marshal's office, Mrs P looked over in quiet disgust at the Marshal as if he'd done something wrong, they entered the Saloon, the smell of liquor and cigar smoke drifted into the air as a man sat down at the bar. A few other people were in the Saloon, some playing poker while others drinking.

The bartender looked up, and said "what can I get ya all," Ms Maria Montez said, "do you have any champagne"? It took him a moment to answer, he hadn't had that before but nodded and went to the back room to see if there was a bottle or two. The Marshal said, "that's on me bartender" and he handed over the money to the bartender, The handsome well-built and well-dressed fellow that came into the Saloon with Ms Maria Montez and the Marshal, he soon realized he was out of his depth and left, Marshal turned to a small group of people and said, "Well now Gentlemen, let me introduce you to Ms Maria Montez she is a fine actress and dancer from the green isle of Ireland." The Governor turned and said, "Oh my, A pleasure to meet you Ms," and the other's followed suit. Without any prompt the town piano player started to play a tune called, 'Within the Cellar's Depth I Sit,' As he played it was unclear whether he knew the rumours that she was the mistress of King of Bavaria, The Marshal promptly went over to the player and said "change the tune son, or its rest of the night behind bars for you," he looked at the Marshal and grinned tipped his cap and then played Rock the Cradle Julie, which was more suited to the crowd. Ms Maria Montez's sat with the gentleman at the table, The Governor who had introduced himself earlier, asked her if she had performed for anyone else of royalty, She replied that she had indeed, She had been given a medal for her dance and song in the presence of a King but didn't disclose which King.

As the night wore on a couple of men approached Ms Maria Montez and said, "You are one beautiful woman, would you like to accompany us tomorrow for a picnic," One of the men was JP he instantly was smitten with her. The other was Sheriff Smith who had already spoken to her and said, "I am looking forward to your performance in Fort Worth." In the morning, Sheriff Smith had the picnic basket ready and a couple of bottles of wine, he then knocked on the Governor's building door but only to be disappointed to see JP answer, He said Thank you Sheriff for your kind gesture with the basket and wine, he took the basket and closed the door. Sheriff Smith stood there in a state of disbelief, his plan was to get the most beautiful woman to spend the day with him. He walked away saddened, and then he thought how JP could do this to me! He wondered back to his office, By this time his wife Shelly was most angry with him and started to cause a scene, The Marshal quickly asked them both to accompany him to his office, when Sheriff Smiff realised what a fool he had been and couldn't apologise to Shelly enough, The Marshal said to them both, "why don't you both go on your own picnic." In the meantime, JP had harnessed the buggy and they both went off for a picnic, enjoying a basket full of delicious homemade goodies. They parked the buggy under a shady tree by a small creek, spread out a blanket, and laid out the food. The sun was high in the sky, casting a warm golden light across the rolling hills and verdant plains, painting the sky in a symphony of vibrant hues., As John looked into Ms. Montez's eyes, he couldn't help but feel a sense of warmth and connection. With a friendly tone in his voice, he gently gazed at her and said, "You know, Ms. Montez, you have a truly captivating way of lighting up a room. Your passion for singing is truly inspiring," following that, they both spent most of the time talking about where they both had come from and the places they had seen and what life was like in America and the Emerald Isle. The sincerity in John's words reflected his genuine appreciation, leaving a smile on both of their faces as they continued their conversation, JP thought he had never met anyone as beautiful and as charming as her, he thought, I must get to know her more, he then asked when do you leave for Fort Worth, she replied the day after tomorrow and then Ms Maria Montez said, "I wish we could have another picnic, but I have to prepare for my performance," As the day went on it was time to head back, as they rode through the warm landscape sharing glances at each other, As they arrived back at Whiteoak's JP escorted her back to the Governor's building, as it now was late, he looked into her eyes and she his, as they were about to say good night, and he to thank her for the day, they both had a sudden urge to embrace each other with both arms, an air of excitement came over the pair and as a reaction, they both kissed passionately , something not usually done in public, this seemed to take an age, but only a minute had passed they both said good night, and JP felt like a million dollars.

The next morning, a few people gathered outside the Governor's building, Ms Maria Montez started to sing, and she sang a song called, 'The Little Grey, her charming voice carried threw the town as she was practicing songs for her performance in Fort Worth, this was a pleasant sound which brought a smile to many people. JP was smitten and wanted to see more of Ms Montez. After her practice, she went to have breakfast at a small café in the town and there she met Mr Thomas from the bank, he promptly invited her to join him and his wife at their home for a small gathering with friends, they discussed a wide range of topics, Including popular songs and theatre, By this time JP was wondering if he would get back out for another picnic and he was getting impatient. As time went on, the morning was nearly over. JP thought that they had found something special in each other, his heart was pounding, waiting for her to appear from Mr Thomas's home, Finally Ms Maria Montez came out of the building, JP approached her and said, "Did you forget we were going on another picnic," "oh sorry," she replied I didn't realise," "the morning had gone so quick," The pair continued to talk for a while Ms Maria Montez wanted to see JP again she said "come with me to Fort Worth?" JP replied "Yes, Yes I will," she then went on to say that the coach was due in the morning, and we will travel together and enjoy each other's company before my performance tomorrow evening, JP agreed and ask if they could meet up later perhaps for dinner, Ms Maria Montez said in a disappointed voice "I'm sorry I have to practice again," but I will meet you in the morning so we can travel together, JP was a little down trodden but didn't let her see it, He went off to his room to pack a small bag, he then decided to take his mind off this, he went off to the Saloon. The saloon was very quiet only a couple of poker players and a drunken cowhand in the corner, The Barkeep ask JP what's your poison Mr?, Whisky he replied. JP Stood there with his whisky on the bar for a while, when Sheriff Smiff came into the Saloon, "Why are you so glum," he said, He looked at Sheriff Smiff and replied, "no reason," knowing his days plans hadn't gone his way. The drunken cowhand then approached the Sheriff and started to agonise him, Sheriff Smiff didn't stand for any nonsense and turned to the drunk and said, "Mister you're spending the rest of the evening in Jail to Sober up," he then turned to JP and asked him to help him take the drunk to Jail.

They Both escorted the drunk to the jail, Sheriff Smiff thanked JP and then went on with his business. JP decided not to go back to the Saloon and went back to his room to read the latest Gazette from Whiteoak's. After reading the front page he turned and saw an article about Ms Montez, The article read, Ms Maria Montez was a unique individual who had a passion for singing and dancing. She spent her days traveling the west, performing in Saloons and Theatres, and she had a special knack for captivating her audience with her voice and her performances. with performances that were always lively and passionate. She sang and danced with a unique style that was all her own. Her voice was sweet and clear, and her dancing was graceful yet energetic. The audience was always mesmerized, and her songs were always met with loud applause. Ms Montez's music touched the hearts of people from all over the west.

She was an inspiration to many, and a testament to the power of music and dance. But then it read, Mr C Rayburn Gentleman and Mine Owner had been courting Ms Maria Montez for several months and later to be engaged to be married. JP didn't believe what he was reading, and he decided to knock on Ms Montez's door but no answer. JP headed off to the Miner's Office to confront them both, but Mr C. Rayburn wasn't there, nor was Ms Montez, He was confused and didn't know what to do next he also knew that Mr C. Rayburn was already married, he wanted to see Ms Maria Montez again for her to explain the article, but he felt like he had been played. The Next morning JP decided not to travel with Ms Maria Montez but to ride out before the coach, and would arrive at Fort Worth, his plan would be to watch Ms Montez's performance, and to see if Mr C. Rayburn would be there too, this would prove the article to be right and he could confront Mr C. Rayburn, he didn't know who was playing who, was Ms Montez, Mr C. Rayburn's mistress, but If he was married why the announcement, so many questions JP had thumping in his head. He left very early before sunup and rode hard so he could arrive at Fort Worth, He hitched his horse and found a place near the theatre to room for the night. He entered the theatre, there where so many people had turned out to see the performance.

After a while JP moved back out of sight so he could observe, Ms Maria Montez captivated the audience with her voice, her performance was exquisite, but he could see a sadness in her eyes after her performance, he managed to get backstage, Mr C Rayburn was nowhere in sight. He knocked on the dressing room door, then an odd-looking tall fellow, very well-dressed, answered the door. JP asked if Ms Maria Montez was available she called "Who is it?" JP gave his name and the gentleman replied back "its JP mam," She then ran to the door with an excitement and a smile on her face, but JP wasn't smiling he just looked confused, Ms Montez's explained that the Gentleman was Ms Montez's manager then she asked him if he would give them a little time together, she said to JP that she thought she was never going to see him again after he didn't turn up for the coach. JP said "I'm sorry I didn't want to be taken in" then he read part of the article, Mr C Rayburn Gentleman and Mine Owner had been courting Ms Maria Montez for several months and they were later to be engaged to be married. Then went on to say to her "I know Mr C Rayburn and he is a married man I thought my intentions was pure"? A tear in Ms Maria Montez eye and she looked quite blushed in the cheeks," she replied It's all been a big mistake I am so sorry how can you forgive me"? Mr C. Rayburn wanted to be my agent, but he got very persuasive, I had no idea he was married, and I feel such a fool now", JP replied and said, "So do I," the pair chatted for a few minutes, they both looked into each other's eyes again and said. Where do we go from here?. Ms Maria Montez said, "I have an idea if you're able to be my companion for my next performance is in New Orleans and I'm expected to be there for several days, If we leave after the next performance tomorrow evening, we could travel together," JP agreed, the pair embraced once again, JP felt excitement of a new adventure. She had told JP to telegraph Whiteoak's and especially Mr C Rayburn to tell him she was heading back to New York. JP thought if Ms Maria Montez plan would work he could spend a lot of time with the girl of his dreams.

The following day JP sent the telegraph and he and Ms Maria Montez spent some time together until it was time for Ms Maria Montez to return to the theatre. While outside the theatre talking a young man approached them, He looked like Tate, JP had only caught sight of Tate a couple of times while he was with Marshal Chapman. Tate had unholstered his pistol, JP was anxious to see that this young fellow was about to point his pistol at him, Ms Maria Montez hugged against JP closely, But then Tate shouted over to them "English Jack raise your arms slowly or I'll fill you full of lead," after this Ms Maria Montez was very frightened, JP called back, "You have the wrong man," the air was tense JP knew if Tate would only listen to him for a few minutes then he would understand that he wasn't English Jack. JP obliged and raised his arms, Tate approached slowly JP said to Ms Maria Montez "This is a misunderstanding and I'll see you later", Ms Maria Montez entered the theatre shaking with fear and then went in to the fetch the manager, but it was too late, Tate had taken JPs pistol and took him along to the Jail, JP still telling Tate that you have the wrong man, All he would reply is that the Judge will see about that. As they arrived at the Jail, a brick building consisted of a strong wooden door and two barred windows, Tate knocked on the door twice the town Sheriff opened the door, there was a large stove in the middle of the room with a coffee pot on and was quite warm, a desk with two chairs, on the wall had an array of wanted posters, then to one side another door way with barred cells, four in total, JP pleaded to the Sheriff and Tate you have the wrong man but without any joy, Tate held up English Jacks wanted poster, it uncannily resembled JP but some sight differences, JP started to fear for his life, as English Jack was wanted for Murder and this crime was punished by death.

JP's cell was nothing but a bunk with a blanket, a bucket in the corner and a strong smell of urine and a stale smell of the Sheriffs cigars, this was very unpleasant , Later on Ms Maria Montez arrived at the Jail and requested to see JP, Tate granted her only a few minutes, JP was relieved to see her, as she approached, the stench of the jail was too much for her, she covered her mouth and nose with a dainty handkerchief to disguise the smell, once at JP's cell JP said "This is a right mess," "I'm so sorry," Ms Maria Montez replied "I know," "the only way I can get out is if you Telegraph Whiteoak's and ask for Marshall Chapman to come in to prove who I am," Ms Maria Montez replied "of course my sweetness," As she left the Jail she hurried to the telegraph office to send the wire. Clearly they had both had fallen for each other, The situation was desperate as Ms Maria Montez was due to catch the morning train to New Orleans, and the Judge was going to try JP. Ms Montez's manager disapproved of their relationship and tried discouraging her from missing the train in the morning to save JP, her testimony could be crucial especially if Marshal Chapman arrives on time. That evening Ms Maria Montez performed again with a sadness in her eyes, but this time JP wasn't there to see her, She left the stage with loud applause. She retired to her room in great sadness, a Knock on the Door it was her manager she told him to go away she didn't want to see anyone. It was a long night Ms Maria Montez spent it in her dressing room, Morning arrived she knew she had two choices to go to the Court house or to catch the train, she knew she had feelings for JP and didn't want any harm to come to him, Her Manager met her outside of the stage door with her bags, again he tried discouraging her not to miss the train and not to go to the courthouse, her emotions had finally won over she turned around to her manager and said, "you're like everyone else only thinking about the money, and not me," He replied, "Suit yourself," She then ran off down the end of the street not looking were she was going, tears rolling down her face, she ran straight into a gentleman nearly knocking him over. He grabbed her arms and said, "Miss do you mind, where are you going in such a hurry", She immediately apologized, As she looked up she saw a familiar face, It was Marshall Chapman, as she wiped her eyes Marshall Chapman recognised her, she felt such relief, As they both stood there she said there's no time to waste, Marshal Chapman said you can explain on the way to the court house, they both hurried Ms Maria Montez explained everything to the Marshal, as they arrived the trial hadn't begun yet he told her to sit down and wait, this was a grand building, the Marshall left and went along a small corridor, this led to rooms at the back of the courthouse, he met up with the District Judge, he explained why he was here, the Judge said if he's not English Jack then he must be released, Marshall agreed, Ms Maria Montez sat on her own in the cold courthouse waiting, by this time the Marshal had gone through the back door and on to the Jail house he approached the Sheriff and deputy Tate, and told them what the Judge had said, The Sheriff said the only way to prove this is to see him, Marshal Chapman approached the cell took one look at JP, JP said "you're a sight for sore eyes thank god you have arrived," Straight away the Marshal turned to the Sheriff and said, "This ain't English Jack," to the relief from JP, The Sheriff open the cell, quickly the Marshal said, "You have someone waiting in the court house," they both left quickly, JP walked through the doors of the courthouse and saw Ms Maria Montez sitting there with her head in her hands sobbing, As he walked down the aisle Ms Maria Montez turned and saw him she got up and ran over to JP embracing him as they hadn't embraced before, Marshal Chapman said "You pair need to hurry if you want to catch the next train, it leaves in an hour", They were so happy to be together again. The Marshal collected their baggage for them and then escorted them both to the station. As the train had left with both of them on it, The Marshal headed back to Whiteoak's he rode up hitched his horse up outside his office, Sheriff Smiff was talking to John Boxx as they were talking, Smiff called over to the Marshal and said, "Where's JP?" the Marshal replied with a smile on his face "We won't see him for a while!" He then turned to enter his office without any explanation. Smiff then looked at Boxx and smiled as he said, "Well, I guess that's that."

Chapter 12

The Hunt for English Jack:

English Jack, a notorious outlaw had emerged from the shadows at Whiteoak's and killed an unarmed man. English Jack had evaded capture by lawmen for some time, leaving a trail of chaos and stolen treasures in his wake, Many were terrified of Jack, for his escapades had made him a legend in the region, He was a skilled marksman with unruly dark hair and piercing blue eyes that seemed to hold many secrets.

Morning had broken, and Tate had returned to Whiteoak's after his mistaken encounter with JP in Fort Worth, He had reported back to the Marshal that English Jack was back in Stenson, The Marshal was determined to find English Jack, With a coffee in one hand he set off to the Court house, He rang the bell for a town meeting to raise a small posse, John Boxx, Tony Whiteoak, Young Tate who recently had recovered from a gunshot wound, and the two Rangers Soapy and Poncho all answered the call, he requested for Sheriff Smiff to stay behind a mind the town in case English Jack tracked back, Smiff obliged with no hesitation, He said to the men to saddle up for lunchtime and take enough provisions for 5 days. They all agreed, Marshall Chapman gathered information from the frightened townsfolk about Jack's whereabouts. Rumours whispered of a hideout deep in the heart of the Pan Handle, a treacherous and perilous terrain that only the bravest dared to explore and close to the territories where Indians were still hostile. Lunchtime arrive and the group were ready to set off, all very capable with a pistol and rifle, Poncho and Soapy's tracking skills in an unforgiving wilderness were second to none as both had been mountain guides and hunters, they all knew that this would be a challenging mission. Chapman issued the order to ride out, the thunder of hooves left the east side of Whiteoak's, some town folks had come out to see what the noise was. After a couple of hours navigating through the unforgiving terrain, battling the scorching heat and the constant threat of danger. Poncho found faint traces left by Jack, like a hawk in pursuit of its prey, but the night was drawing in and it was time to make camp, they all agreed, Tony said he would keep first watch as many had died in these parts from Indian and Bandit attacks. The rest settled up, Tate sorted the horses, John lit a small fire and got the Coffee pot on, Marshal Chapman stood gazing out towards the darkness, he knew that he was in pursuit of the one of the most dangerous men he ever had to face, As the Mesquite trees cast shadows around the campfire, sounds of the wilderness echoed through the wind, John, Tate and Soapy listened to Poncho, telling stories about his mountain adventures with his rugged charm, A couple of hours passed and it was John's turn to keep watch, soon, morning came and it was time to pick up the faint trail. After they had freshened up and saddled up Poncho picked up the trail, but his skills were soon put to the test, as Jack seemed to anticipate his every move, leaving decoys along the way, He turned to Marshal Chapman and said, "This one is a quite a cunning fellow like a fox!" The Marshal nodded his head and continued to follow the trail.

Tate, John and Tony in the rear could see dark clouds in the distance as Soapy, Poncho and Chapman were deep following the trail, Tate with a heel on his horse rode up beside Chapman and said, "there's a storm coming and we need to take shelter," Tony called out "I know of a place not far from here, there's an abandoned place 10 miles to the west, we can see the storm out from there," they soon arrived at the ranch just as Tony had said, Tony and John dismounted and started to anxiously peer through the windows in case any unwanted guests were there. Nobody had lived in the old ranch for years. Situated amidst the vast expanse of a rugged western landscape, the dusty old ranch that seemed frozen in time. With its weathered wooden beams and old fireplace covered in dust, this place exudes a certain sense of authenticity that can only be found in the lore of the Wild West, as whispers of war tales and triumphs and sadness still linger in the wind. Despite its aging appearance, the ranch still carries a timeless charm that captivates each of the men. John turned to Tony and said, "how do you know of this place?" Tony replied, "some years ago I stopped here," but he didn't divulge any more to John, John looked over to Tony and smiled, then said, "I guess we all have our secrets." As the sun started to set, it painted the sky with fiery hues, casting a warm glow upon the ranch's worn corral and barn, but soon the ominous storm clouds in the distance started to move closer. The storm was about to hit, the sound of thunder, intense rainfall, strong winds, they knew it would be a long night, The rain started to leak through the old roof and onto the wooden floor, making a puddle beneath them. They huddled together, the warmth of each other's bodies providing a small comfort in the midst of this chaos. They looked around the small, dilapidated building, its walls barely holding together against the onslaught of the storm. Poncho said, "any clues will be washed out by tomorrow and we would have to start again," Chapman replied, "Is that's so, English Jack wouldn't be able to get far either," Just after that Chapman said to Tate, "go and check the horses, make sure the tethered in for the storm." But something was bothering Chapman, John and Tony both looked across the room at Chapman to ask him what the matter was, as the heavy rain poured down relentlessly, creating a sombre harmony with the desolate landscape.

Amidst the downpour, suddenly a sharp clap of thunder which sounded like a gunshot echoed through the air, shattering the eerie calmness that prevailed. The reverberations filled the atmosphere, evoking a sense of mystery and trepidation, Chapman turned to John and Tony and called out "Tate," but it was too late, Tate lay sprawled on the wet ground, Chapman looked on out of the broken window in horror, as it wasn't thunder it was a gunshot, he was unsure whether this was English Jack or someone else, but Tate was dead on the ground, there was a weight of regret and loss hung in the air,

John said to Tony "That could have been any of us", "Sure it could have," he replied, they both went outside with their rifles, only to find the assailant had gone, The tracks in the mud showed two horses. An air of desperation had set in as they needed to get back out to track English Jack, and Tates Killer, Chapman said We will ride first light, someone keep watch as the killer could return, that night nobody could sleep, dawn broke and a mist of damp air rose, Chapman said, "I will bury Tate," It was as if the hunter had become hunted. Marshal Chapman went over to Tate, He lay motionless on the wet ground with a single gunshot to the chest, the pungent smell of wet earth mingling with an unmistakable air of sorrow, Tates death lay heavy with Marshal Chapman, as the weight of choices made in this harsh and lawless land are difficult, one could not help but ponder the paths not taken and the lives cut short in this desolate land.

The Marshal dug a grave around the side of the ranch, Soapy, Poncho, John and Tony stood overlooking with sadness, Soapy said should we say something? John turned and said "We gather here today in grief to remember the life of Tate, taken too young and to support one another during this difficult time. As we come together, let us take a moment to offer a prayer of comfort, healing, and strength, Amen." Tony looked at John and nodded his head in an appreciation of his kind words, Chapman covered the rest of the grave with some rocks and made a cross from some old wood from the barn. After he said to Soapy and Poncho, you two need to follow those new tracks of the two horses, Me, John, and Tony will try and pick up from before the storm.

We will meet back here in two days. They loaded the rest of the supplies on Tates horse, and the band of men separated. Tracking an elusive outlaw could test even the most seasoned lawman's resolve. Marshal Chapman, renowned for his unwavering dedication to justice, As they embarked on the treacherous pursuit alongside his trusted allies, Tony and John. However, as they hiked through the desolate landscapes, the trail inexplicably went dry, leaving them at a vexing crossroad. Undeterred, the trio of men meticulously combed through every lead and clue, expertly piecing together fragments of information in their relentless pursuit of the fugitive.

With a professional tone, Marshal Chapman meticulously analysed their next steps, employing his vast experience to devise a strategic plan that would breathe life back into the seemingly barren investigation. Guided by a steely determination, these seasoned men were an indomitable force, resolute in their mission to bring this outlaw to justice and restore tranquillity to the troubled frontier. As the day went on they felt they were getting closer, but evening was drawing in Marshal Chapman, Tony, and John needed to set up camp for the night, As dusk settled and the temperature dropped Marshal Chapman built a campfire which provided warmth, the coffee pot was nearly ready as Tony, with his keen eye for detail, arranged the saddles and blankets, ensuring comfort and a restful night's sleep. Meanwhile, John adeptly set up a perimeter, securing the campsite and keeping a watchful eye on their surroundings. It was a clear night with no clouds, The Marshal, John, and Tony found themselves gathered around a campfire, creating an atmosphere of sombreness.

Despite the bright stars lighting up the sky, a sense of gravity hung in the air as the flickering flames cast dancing shadows on their faces as they still reflected on Tate, Marshal Chapman, John, and Tony found solace in the quietude of the night, allowing them to reflect and find comfort in each other's presence. After diligently tracking the elusive English Jack, Marshal Chapman, John, and Tony reluctantly concluded that the trail had gone cold. With the understanding of their line of work, they knew that sometimes even the most careful investigations could hit dead ends, Exercising their keen judgement and expertise, they made the decision to head back to the ranch, regroup, and reevaluate their strategy while they wait for Soapy and Poncho to return. The Marshal was still dwelling on the frustration of the situation, and he couldn't help thinking he had failed. After riding for most of the day, the men neared the ranch, Marshal Chapman could see two horses, but they weren't Poncho's or Soapy's, cautiously they approached, a single figure came out of the ranch door heavily armed, the air was heavy with tension as they prepared for what lay ahead. The Marshal, John and Tony was armed and knew how to use them, acutely aware of the potential dangers that awaited them inside. They moved silently, their professional instincts guiding their every step. As they neared the figure, their senses sharpened, their focus honed. They knew that this encounter could be pivotal on what happens next. Chapman shouted out with a raised voice to proclaim his presence, asserting, "I'm Marshal Chapman, and these men by my side are my trusted deputies," With an air of unwavering confidence, he made it clear that he was in charge.

As he moved closer Tony moved away and John moved to the side so he could encircle, A rifle barrel could be seen through the broken window, Marshal Chapman again shouted out with a raised voice, the heavily armed man, adrenaline pumping through his veins, answered in a Hispanic resolute tone. In that moment, a fleeting sense of relief washed over Marshal Chapman, knowing that his words had been heard and understood amidst the pandemonium. But suddenly a folly of gun fire came from the window, the bullets pierced through the tense atmosphere, they sliced through the air with a menacing swiftness. The precision with which they narrowly missed the Marshal was a chilling testament to the unskilled marksmanship of those who sought to silence him. In that moment, the gravity of the situation became palpable, underscoring the dangers inherent in his role as a Marshal. Chapman instantly knew these men were bandits and weren't going to give up without a fight, a surge of adrenaline coursed through Chapman's veins, fuelling his resolve. The weight of his duty bore heavily on his shoulders, and he knew that these men had killed Tate, like a man of steel Marshal Chapman and his companions drew their pistols.

 The Marshall with his trusted dragoon a 44, Tony with his 73 colt and another 44, and John with his two Colts, Their pistols, gleaming in the sunlight, became an extension of their unwavering resolve, In unison, they took aim, with a resolute determination etched upon their faces. From their every gesture and hardened expressions, one could discern the discipline and expertise that had been ingrained through countless moments of experience. As the smoke cleared, revealing the chaotic aftermath, the figures of the two bandits emerged, The air was thick with tension as their cold steel was on the ground they both had been gunned down, the Marshal and his two companions with each step they took, a sense of controlled confidence emanated from them, sending shivers down the spines of those unlucky enough to cross their path. They were not merely common criminals, These two bandits that had just been vanquished, they were members of the notorious Antonio's gang, an infamous menace that had been causing havoc throughout the region.

Their elimination was no small feat and Marshal Chapman was relieved the commotion was over, under his breath his said, "I'm too old for this." This wasn't the first time that the Marshal had encountered bandits from Antonios gang, the last time Tate was wounded in the leg, 13 miles out of Whiteoak's, in the distance two riders began to make their appearance. It became clear that the figures in question were none other than Soapy and Poncho. However, one couldn't help but ponder over the fact that they had regrettably missed a crucial point in time.

They greeted the Marshal as he and the others had collected the warm bodies and placed them upon their horses, slumped over the saddle face down, Poncho lifted the head of one and said, these two are members of Antonios gang, It looks like Miguel and Carlos, their involvement in criminal activities has caused the District judge in Fort Worth to issue warrants. The warrants stand as a testament to the serious nature of their offences and the importance of holding them accountable for their actions. Soapy and Poncho said to the Marshal, "We will take these into Fort Worth, if you don't mind," The Marshal then replied, "Once you have finished that assignment, we will regroup at Whiteoak's." Then he went on to say that "It appears that the trail left by English Jack has gone cold." Clear and concise, Marshal conveyed a sense of urgency and maintained a level-headed approach to the situation. Marshal Chapman, Tony, and John, swiftly gathered their horses, preparing to embark on their journey back to Whiteoak's. Each man exuded a stoic determination as they tightened their saddle straps and ensured their equipment was in perfect order before their journey. They mounted their horses, the rhythmic clinks of their spurs echoing through the stillness. As they set off, their actions were calculated and deliberate, a testament to their years of experience in this rugged terrain and set off knowingly it was at least two days ride. Marshal chapman John and Tony arrived back at Whiteoak's, They rode through the streets, a tangible air of resolve surrounded them. The townsfolk watched with admiration as they rode with purpose, The Marshal's badge glinting in the sunlight. This courageous trio had just completed a daunting mission but without sorrow, as there was one rider missing, Young Tate. Marshal Chapman John and Tony were not just symbols of law and order; they were living embodiments of the unwavering dedication that upholds the peace and safety of Whiteoak's. but it also signified the commencement of a fresh chapter. However, the persistent presence of English Jack, who had managed to evade capture, cast a shadow of uncertainty over this newfound sense of security. The Marshal knew eventually peace and tranquillity would prevail. Tony and John went back to their normal Jobs Tony a gunsmith and John proprietor of the Assays office, and then the Marshal set off to his own office with and air of sadness in his heart. His wife met him at the door, aware of his emotional state, She awaited him with open arms and a loving smile. In that poignant moment, their eyes locked, and the unspoken understanding between them provided solace for Marshal's troubled mind. "I was so worried about you," she said, her voice shaking with concern. "What happened out there?" As he related the events of the past few days, she listened intently, her expression growing increasingly grave. Her eyes darted around the room, as if searching for answers in the familiar surroundings. When he finished, she reached up and cupped his cheek in her hand, her thumb brushing away a stray tear.

Chapter 13

Who Shot Bubba (The Town Mayor):

As Sheriff Smith received the urgent message summoning him to a shooting incident in main street of Whiteoak's, the adrenaline coursing through his veins electrified his senses. The gravity of the situation hung heavy in the air as he made his way swiftly to the scene. uncertainty gripped him. The identity of the victim, who was barely clinging to life, still remained unknown to him. This tense situation took an even more dire turn when it was revealed that the victim was the town Mayor. With quick senses the Doc was fetched with much urgency, A small buggy quickly transported the Mayor to the surgeon's house, then upon the operating table, The slug had pierced deep into his flesh, causing blood to steadily flow out from the wound. Time was of the essence, and every second that ticked away meant a further loss of blood – a further decline in the chances of his survival, it was up to the Doc, the key to his salvation, and to deliver him from this perilous state. Doc skilfully performed surgery on the Mayor, but there were tense moments as the Mayor drifted in and out of consciousness, with only whisky to quash his pain, his strength had been sapped by a gunshot wound to the lower abdomen. The Doc performed many such operations during the war years despite the inherent risks, Doc utilized his extensive expertise and unwavering commitment to save as many lives as possible, but the outcome was often the latter.

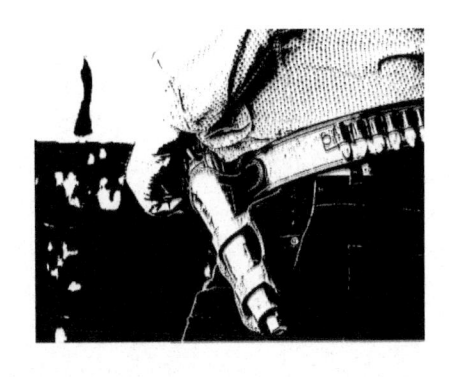

Bubba the Town Mayor wasn't out of the woods yet, he had to stay with the Doc, and the next 24 hours were crucial for his survival. Although the Town Mayor, Bubba owned Brokenwood Mercantile along with Ms Kate, his partner. Sheriff Smith summoned Ms. Kate to stand by Bubba's side, signalling the onset of an arduous night ahead. The two of them sat in the dimly lit room, the only light filtering through the curtained windows, casting long shadows across the dusty floorboards. The silence was palpable, thick with unspoken fears and uncertainties. They both knew that if Bubba didn't make it, the future of Brokenwood would be thrown into disarray. Sheriff Smith knowing nothing else could be done he retired back to his office, questioning in himself who would want the Mayor dead? Who is the assailant? So many questions, and so many angles the shot could have been fired from. He needed to find the cartridge case if there was one. He waited until morning to gather the evidence and start to piece together events. It was evident earlier in the year that Bubba was crucial in determining whether he can continue his reign as Town Mayor, Smiff thought this would be a good place to start.

He looked back at the writings of the Gazette to remind him the events leading up and towards the Mayors campaign and vote, we go back in time to earlier in the year. Whiteoak's, a charismatic frontier town, embarked on an exhilarating journey as they held their highly anticipated elections, electrifying political adventure as the campaign kickstarts in May, paving the way for the buzzing June Elections, It was scheduled to take place in the iconic Court House during the exciting week of the following month. The town braced itself for the forthcoming clash of ideologies, as candidates and voters alike gear up to embark on this monumental journey of democracy. Whiteoak's previous elections, which had been rather lacklustre and uneventful, suddenly veered onto a different path. Breaking free from the monotony of the past, an adventurous energy surged through the community as daring candidates stepped forward, ready to challenge the status quo. The atmosphere crackled with anticipation, as an air of excitement enveloped the town. The once-familiar faces of the same elected officials were now met with murmurs of intrigue and curiosity. It seemed as though Whiteoak's political landscape was about to undergo a captivating transformation, ready to embark on a thrilling journey of change. This year ushered in a wave of fresh faces in the political arena, brimming with Vigor and determination. These new candidates have brought an adventurous spirit to the forefront of discussions, For many didn't want change, this year candidates were as follows: Governor - Mr Atwal (Republican) Governors Assistant - Mr A Whiteoak (Republican) Mr J Boxx (Republican) Town Mayor - Bubba (Republican) Mr JD Rayburn (Republican) Senor Miguel (Democrat) Town Clerk - Vacant No Candidates, Town Buildings and Construction Committee Mr J Boxx (Republican) Mr P West (Republican) Mr Adams (Democrat) Town Sheriff -Mr Smiff (Democrat) Mr A Lawdog (Democrat) Marshal - Mr A Chapman (Republican) Town Treasurers Thomas Trust & Savings Bank Head Cashier Mrs P,& Mr Thomas (Republican) Head of Sanitary Mr D Thomas (Republican) Fire Committee- - Mr J Boxx , Mr A Whiteoak, Bubba, Livestock Committee Mr London, Mr Lonesome, Triple RR Cattle Company. Ms M Williams Stenson Ranch. For those who didn't have an opponent they were to be re-elected by default.

The canvassing had begun, in particular Town Mayor - Bubba (Republican) Mr JD Rayburn (Republican) Senor Miguel (Democrat) Already under suspicion was Mr JD Rayburn as he sent his brother, Mr. Cole Rayburn embarked on his canvassing journey, the weeks progressed, and an air of excitement and uncertainty enveloped the town. Whispers of change began to circulate amongst the residents, fuelling speculation that perhaps the days of the Town Mayor were numbered. As polling day approached, excitement filled the air. Judge Pee, the trusted overseer of the ballot box, and Sheriff Smiff, the vigilant guardian of proper proceedings, were ready to carry out their crucial roles, Sheriff Smiff to ensure the Thirteenth, Fourteenth and Fifteenth amendment to the constitution extended civil and legal protection to former slaves to have their vote, however some states still deny black citizens of their legal rights, Sheriff Smiff will ensure that there will be no wrongdoing during the ballot when it's held. Marshal Chapman's presence on the doorsteps of the courthouse serves as a formidable symbol of justice and safety. With his stern demeanour and unwavering dedication to upholding the law, he effectively persuades both passersby and potential wrongdoers that the court's authority will not be undermined. As the vote went on the results were declared Governor - Mr Atwal no change Assistant

Governor - Mr A Whiteoak, Re- Elected, Town Mayor – Bubba Western - Re-Elected, Town Clerk – Vacant, Town Buildings and Construction Committee -Mr J Boxx - Re-Elected, Town Sheriff - Trooper Smiff Re-Elected, Marshal – Mr A Chapman Re-elected, Town Treasurer- Thomas Trust & Savings Bank Head Cashier Mrs P, Re- elected, Head of Sanitary - Mr D Thomas Re-elected, Assistant Sanitary – Mr Smiff ,Fire Committee- - J Boxx , A Whiteoak, Bubba Re -elected. Livestock Committee - Ms M Williams Elected. Sadley not much had changed within the structure of Democratic Whiteoak's.

Shortly after the poling day the Town Mayors birthday was cut short, In a town plagued by rumours and shadows, Sheriff Smiff's sudden absence created a void that needed to be filled. Little did anyone know that Marshal Chapman, a seasoned lawman with a steely gaze and a heart of adventure, Marshals were notorious for their tenacity and their unwavering commitment to justice, and Chapman was no exception. The air was thick with tension as he delved into the web of allegations against the Town Mayor, accusations of corruption and election rigging that had cast doubt over the integrity of the entire community, In an unusual turn of events, Bubba, the esteemed Town Mayor, discreetly arrived at the local jail accompanied by the steadfast Marshal. Due to the Sheriff's absence as mandated by the law, an unexpected twist unfolded – Bubba found himself facing trial. Despite the mayor's usually composed demeanour, this unforeseen circumstance undoubtedly presented a challenge. Engaging with the legal proceedings, Bubba and the Marshal approached the jail quietly, showcasing the importance of maintaining order and upholding the law, Due to the extended absence of the Sheriff, who wouldn't be available for several weeks, the trial was faced with an urgent dilemma - time was of the essence. Understanding the gravity of the situation, the Marshal swiftly stepped in, ensuring that the wheels of justice kept turning. Acting on behalf of the plaintiff and armed with the allegations at hand, the Marshal took charge.

The day of reckoning arrived, Bubba, accompanied by law enforcement, was ceremoniously transported from the confines of the jail to the solemn setting of the courthouse. A sizeable crowd had assembled outside, their collective voices echoing through the air as they enthusiastically expressed their divergent opinions about the Mayor. They alternated between a cacophony of jeers and chants, both in support and against the embattled politician. Inside, Judge Pee, resolute and undeterred by the uproar, was fully prepared to preside over this consequential trial and tackle any challenges that may arise. A jury had been thoughtfully chosen through a process of random selection, ensuring a fair and impartial judgment of justice. With the stage set. JP McCrae, a highly accomplished lawyer with a strong background in law, was chosen to represent Bubba, and Marshal Chapman to read out the allegations on behalf of the plaintiff. The trial had only just started when the crowd outside the courthouse supporting the Mayor soon became angry, Amidst the uproar and chaos that was brewing outside the courthouse, the situation had escalated to a point where the intervention of the Marshal was inevitable. Grasping the gravity of the escalating commotion, the Marshal made a decisive move by stepping outside, willing to confront the relentless crowd. The demands echoed through the air, with the multitude fervently seeking the release of the Mayor.

As the situation intensified, with ruffians indiscriminately shooting into the air, tensions reached a breaking point. Recognizing the need for reinforcements, the Marshal urgently dispatched a message to Ranger Soapy, who was known for his ability to handle unruly crowds. Both lawmen understood that the odds were stacked against them, as they were greatly outnumbered and could not rely on the hesitant townsfolk for assistance. Showing remarkable composure, they discharged their own firearms as a warning, attempting to disperse the unruly crowd and restore order.

During the course of the trial, amidst all that was happening, Judge Pee had to confront the unsettling circumstances surrounding the case. JP McCrae, the defence attorney, diligently carried on, dismissing some of the allegations as false and passionately pleading with the jury to consider Bubba's innocence. However, as tensions escalated, the judge was forced to acknowledge the growing mob outside the courtroom, their presence creating an unsettling atmosphere. In a professional manner, Judge Pee turned to the jury and proposed the option to adjourn the case, understanding the need for a calm and unbiased deliberation. It was a moment where both justice and public safety had to be carefully weighed, reminding everyone present of the gravity and responsibility that rested upon their shoulders. Despite any potential reservations, the Jury had already unanimously voted to deliver a guilty verdict for the Mayor. Consequently, Judge Pee found herself in a predicament, compelled to uphold the jury's decision and subsequently pronounce the Mayor guilty. Regrettably, the gravity of the situation necessitated Judge Pee to sentence the Mayor to hang, leaving the judge with no room to exercise leniency. In adherence to his duty, the Marshal dutifully escorted the Mayor to the Gallows, Then out of the crowd a woman approached the Marshal, claiming she was carrying Bubba's child, she claimed she was from Oklahoma, then another appeared stating she was from Arkansas, again claiming to be with child, then a bizarre thing happened next a rugged man came forward claiming he was in love with the Mayor, and he claimed he was from Los Angeles. Bubba's wife was in dismay and didn't know who to turn to or believe, The event can only be described as an utter fiasco. Amidst chaos and confusion, the representative for defendant, JP McCrae desperately pleaded for bail at the Gallows, hoping for a chance of a retrial. Astonishingly, Judge Pee granted this request right before the rope was meant to be put around the Mayors' neck. Despite attempting to maintain a professional tone, it is difficult to overlook the glaring mishandling of this situation. After careful consideration of the circumstances, the Judge ultimately deemed it appropriate to set bail at one thousand dollars for Bubba's case. However, there was an unexpected turn of events when a mysterious donor stepped forward to cover the entire sum. As a result, Bubba was able to regain his freedom until the retrial. Surprisingly, the announcement of the donor's gesture caused the crowd to disperse without any incident or commotion, Due to the extensive involvement of the majority of the town's residents in the incident, the task of the Marshal to enforce any disciplinary measures under the law proved to be quite challenging. With numerous individuals implicated, distinguishing the culpable parties from the innocent became a complex task, warranting a re-trial that has been scheduled for September.

September's trial arrived the Town Mayor again was due to appear in court but due a lack of new evidence to support the plaintiff's complaint, Judge Pee has yet again to re-evaluate the case as the situation remained the same, and Judge Pee had no choice to adjourn, But the Mayor was still on bail. Judge Pee made a statement that "it's possible that the corruption and rigging of the election could have been down to the plaintiff," who still remains a mystery and hasn't returned to town. Judge Pee made a noteworthy statement regarding the plaintiff's absence in the upcoming trial. Emphasizing the importance of the plaintiff's presence, the Judge asserted that failing to appear would inevitably lead to the dismissal of all charges brought forth in the plaintiff's complaint. This decision would effectively favour the Mayor's position in the case.

Back to the present, Sheriff Smith, armed with the background information from the Gazette, necessary for his investigation, he's determination to find Bubba's assailant, Sheriff Smiff meticulously searched every inch of the street in an attempt to locate an empty cartridge case, Despite the lack of success in finding the object of his search, As he made his way through the streets of Whiteoak's, he couldn't help but notice the intrigued glances from the townsfolk. They had heard rumours and whispers of the mysterious events unfolding but were mostly unaware of the gravity of the situation. This was his moment, the time to dive deep into the heart of the matter. With a persuasive tone and unwavering determination As Smiff prepared to question his key suspects, JD Cole and his brother, he adopted a persuasive tone of voice. Aware of the gravity of the situation, Smiff, skilfully approached the interrogation, determined to unravel the truth, But JD Cole's only admission was that he had broken the poling regulations for canvasing and pretending to be his brother, Senor Miguel, the master of adding fuel to the fire! Just when we thought the case couldn't get any more dramatic, he swoops in with his wild story, like a twist from wild winds.

Sheriff Smiff found himself utterly perplexed when confronted with the puzzling possibility that his opponent, a fellow candidate for the race of candidacy, had purportedly received a substantial amount of money to gracefully withdraw from the competition. As he fervently scrutinized the evidence at hand, it became increasingly clear that something didn't quite add up. The situation was as confounding as trying to fit a square peg into a round hole with the finesse of a clumsy circus performer. Sheriff Smiff, renowned for his quick wit and astute observations, couldn't help but chuckle inwardly at the audacity of it all. He pondered on the whimsical notion that perhaps his opponent had been rendered a hefty sum of gold coins in an attempt to slyly slink away from the spotlight. With eyebrows raised and a wry smile tugging at his lips, Sheriff Smiff resolved to uncover the truth behind this curious case.

As Bubba's investigation continued, the puzzling question of who desired his removal lingered in his mind. With each suspect eliminated, the pool grew shallower, making the enigma even more intriguing. The mysterious man who bailed Bubba out of jail added further complication to the situation. Who was this enigmatic figure, and what was their connection to Bubba's troubles? The peculiarity escalated when a note mysteriously appeared, nonchalantly pushed through the Sheriff's door. The note highlighting names unknown to the Sheriff, he walked across the Street to see who the messenger was, but nobody was in sight, he knocked on the Marshal's door to see if he recognised any of the names on the note, but the Marshal had no idea too, but he did say he would wire the district Judges office in Fort Worth.

Smiff, usually unfazed by such incidents, found himself genuinely bewildered. The intricate web of events had everyone scratching their heads, wondering just what kind of game was being played. It was a captivating conundrum that kept minds racing and tongues wagging in Whiteoak's.

Who were the two women that emerged, each claiming to be carrying Bubba's children, but both mysteriously vanished thereafter, and the rugged man again disappeared after the trial? This puzzling turn of events added yet another layer of complexity to who Shot Bubba? Sheriff Smiff, diligently embarked on the task of deciphering the mysteries that had befallen Whiteoak's. With a firm resolve and unwavering determination, one by one, meticulously probing for any hints or elusive clues that might unravel the enigmatic situation at hand. He asked thought-provoking questions, seeking to shed light on the perplexity that had gripped the community. Many conversations went by without any noteworthy revelations, until finally, a breakthrough emerged. A witness, previously reticent, finally disclosed a crucial piece of information that had eluded others. Nearing closer to the plaintiff identity who he believed to be the cause of the trial and to be the assailant. He's main suspects Cole Rayburn, Jeb, and Poncho a Ranger who recently had a disagreement with Bubba, and Senor Miguel, with the unknown names on the note.

As the day drew near its end, the sun transformed the sky into a breathtaking canvas of warm hues, the evening casting long shadows on the streets of Whiteoak's, Oil lamps lit the streets, a mix of anticipation and concern filled the air. Sheriff Smiff, in his role as a diligent law enforcement officer, knew that it was crucial to stay updated on the progress of Bubba, given the challenging circumstances they had recently faced in the last 24 hours. The Sheriff headed back to the Doc's, he reassured Smiff that Bubba would make it, and he could return home the day after tomorrow. Smiff with the satisfaction of the knowledge the bubba was now safe he could retire until the morning, and reconvene the investigation, As he was heading back up the main street, a shiny piece of metal caught his eye in the moonlight. The glimmering object stood out amidst the darkness, casting a mesmerizing reflection, it was a cartridge case from a small calibre, this meant that the assailant was close when they took the shot. Despite its claim of being a 36, the size of the gun, Smiff seemed more appropriate for the attack would be a derringer or a small pocket pistol. However, Smiff's confidence unaverred as he recognized the crucial role this seemingly inadequate weapon would play in his investigation.

As morning arrived, Sheriff Smiff emerged from his slumber feeling refreshed and ready to tackle the task at hand. He rose bright and early, eager to solve the perplexing case that had consumed his thoughts, He greeted Marshal Chapman as he was about to do his rounds, the pair engaged in conversation about the complex case, John suddenly interrupted them to announce that he had just received a wire from Fort Worth District Judges office. A Silence drew as Chapman and Smiff eagerly turned their attention towards him. Could this be the breakthrough that Smiff had been waiting for? Who or what was on the wire? Smiff confidently grasped the wire in his capable hands, ready to unravel the mysteries hidden within its intricate web. As his eyes scanned the written words, he instinctively began to read aloud, names as follows - J Carter currently serving a 10-year sentence at Huntsville Texas State Penitentiary and Jack Slater ……. wanted for embezzlement and fraud. The following was a revelation, and this was certainly the breakthrough he needed, as Jack Slater was a close friend of Senor Miguel. Marshal Chapman knew that he was in town when the attempt on Bubba's life had taken place, Jack Slater was also present at the elections. But Senor Miguel was the Doc's assistant, the pair needed to rush to the Doc's quickly with no hesitation, Sheriff Smiff and Marshal Chapman headed toward the Doc's house. As the pair approached the house, the Doc greeted them on the front porch, However, the air quickly grew tense as Sheriff Smiff intervened, his voice stern and commanding. He made it clear that their presence at the location was solely for Senor Miguel. However, to his surprise, he calmly replied that Senor Miguel was not present. As it turned out, he had ridden off to the Broken Barrel with Jack. This was an old trading post near the border, this was situated west of Whiteoak's, a place that required several days of travel to reach, Marshal Chapman knew that in this establishment, rogues gathered from time to time and also weary travellers. The Doc followed on to say that they were meeting a rogue known as 'Dealer'.

The Marshal and Sheriff, being well-versed in the delicate art of law enforcement, were acutely aware of the potential repercussions that would arise from riding to the infamously rowdy Broken Barrel with a posse in tow. Their experienced eyes had seen firsthand how such actions could stir up a hornet's nest of trouble that could quickly spiral out of control. Wisely, the astute duo reached a consensus, recognizing that a more prudent course of action would be to exercise patience and lie in wait until the opportune moment to make their move. After several days of waiting, Senor Miguel and Jack Slater finally rode back into town. As they approached, they couldn't shake off a feeling of unease. There was an unusual air of anticipation in the usually quiet streets. To their surprise, awaiting their arrival were none other than Sheriff Smith and Marshal Chapman, with a determined look on their faces ready to arrest them. As Sheriff Smiff read their charges Senor Miguel's eyes widened in disbelief. "Sheriff, you can't be serious! You know we'd never do such a thing." Marshal Chapman interjected, his voice stern and unwavering. However, all eyes turned to Jack, who, unable to contain his fear, made an ill-advised dash for freedom, quick of the mark Marshal Chapman caught Jack with ease. While in the town jail, awaiting transportation to the district Judge for trial, Senor Miguel and Jack found themselves facing the weight of their past actions. With a sombre understanding of the consequences, they were about to face, they made the decision to confess. Sheriff Smiff was ready to hear all, the conclusion to this sordid tale.

Jack Slater had served time with J Carter at Huntsville It was during their time behind bars that they hatched a daring scheme that would forever etch their names in the annals of audacity. With eyes glittering with the lustrous sparkle of a silver mine's riches, they meticulously devised an elaborate plan to rob its legendary strongbox. While Carter still in prison and upon Jack's release, he found an old friend Senor Miguel he would meet him at the notorious Broken Barrel out post, Where Jack had gone through the elaborate plan with Senor Miguel offering him gold coins to go along with it, the robbery was to take place with all the confusion on the arrest and trial of Bubba the town mayor, the pair also rigged the election, Jack Slater had paid off Cole unaware of his own mine was about to be robbed, Jack Slater also being the mysterious plaintiff, being out of town couldn't be a part of the scheme, everything was going to plan, even down to paying two working girls to pose as carrying child on the day of trial and gave an old vagabond a couple of dollar's to play his part. He then admitted in amidst the whirlwind of chaos unfolding, Senor Miguel and Jack seized a moment of opportunity, stealthily infiltrating the Mines office with hearts pounding and adrenaline coursing through their veins. Their objective? Retrieve the highly coveted strong box. However, fate had a wicked sense of humour as J Carter, the mischievous mastermind, had unknowingly misled them with erroneous information regarding the day. As they prised open the box, time seemed to stand still, only to reveal a devastating realization of 'emptiness'. Undeterred the pair rejoined the chaos of the trial. At this point Mr Whiteoak heard the pair had been arrested and entered the Sheriff's office to confess he had put up the bail for Bubba as he didn't want to see an old friend hang.

As the eerie silence settled over the room, the Sheriff's eyes narrowed, and he posed the crucial question that hung heavy in the air: "Who shot Bubba?" Jack Slater answered, "Me," The Sheriff gasped in disbelief, his scepticism evident. "You're not a killer?" he replied, struggling to comprehend the situation. Jack shrugged, his rogue nature seeping through his words. "A rogue, yes," he admitted, and I tried to Kill Bubba.

In the midst of their exhilarating encounter, Sheriff's curiosity peaked as he questioned the unexpected revelation of Bubba stumbling upon his true identity as the plaintiff. With a mischievous glint in his eyes, he couldn't help but wonder who had penned the enigmatic note that Senor Miguel reluctantly took responsibility for. Senor Miguel hung his head in a mix of embarrassment and uncertainty before sheepishly admitting, "I wrote the note, and the Doc delivered it, Sheriff. I figured those who were tailing us would be thrown off our trail if they thought someone else was pulling the strings." The admission reflected the daring nature of their escapades.

As dawn broke the following day, Senor Miguel and Jack Slater found themselves unceremoniously loaded into the prison wagon, like two peas in a very unfortunate pod. The exchange of glances between them spoke volumes, a mix of resignation and a barely concealed hint of mischievousness. They left for Fort Worth and that was the last Whiteoak's saw of Jack and Senor Miguel, Later the Marshal had received a wire to say the district Judge sentenced Jack to Hang and Senor Miguel life at Huntsville Texas State Penitentiary.

After what seemed like an eternity, the case was finally over, and Sheriff Smiff, felt a wave of relief wash over him. However, there was one loose end that needed tying up. He headed off to the Doc's house, The Doc had fled knowing his integrity would be in question and would not to be seen again, leaving behind a twinge of disappointment, Sheriff Smiff knew he had to press on. Smiff couldn't help but wonder what drove The Doc to commit such a crime with Senor Miguel. Was it desperation, greed, or something deeper? The thought troubled him, but he pushed it aside and continued back to his Office.

Chapter 14

The Siege Of Whiteoak's:

This was the day, soaked in anticipation and brimming with adventure, when Bandit Antonio decided to unleash his vengeance upon the people of Whiteoak's. With a gleam in his eye and a wild grin on his rugged face, he embarked on a daring quest to settle the score with Sheriff Smiff and Marshal Chapman once and for all. Antonio believed he had been wronged by the lawmen of Whiteoak's, his name tarnished with in the circles of outlaws such as Chucho el Roto, Heraclio Bernal just to name two, with his pride shattered, but no longer would he be the victim in this treacherous game. Armed with his wits, a touch of unpredictability, and an unwavering determination, he and his men set out on a relentless pursuit through the rugged terrain, Their hearts full of anticipation, they neared the infamous Deadman's Finger, a mere thirteen miles away from the bustling town of Whiteoak's. The thrill of the chase electrified their every move as they faced the challenges.

All the men were heavily armed as they were setting out for war and the thrill of the chase guided their every move toward the inevitable clash on the battlefield which would be Whiteoak's. Antonio, the bold and fearless leader, gazed upon the treacherous terrain ahead and made a commanding decision - it was time for his weary men to halt their expedition and seek solace at Deadman's Finger as many did before him, they had been riding for many days from the boarder of Mexico, His gang was an eclectic mix of men, each with their unique stories and backgrounds, some just cattle and horse rustlers, others downright murderous soles, In the vast and rugged landscape,

Bandit Antonio emerged as a formidable figure, leading his daring band of men on adrenaline-fueled escapades. With his half-Mexican heritage, he possessed a fiery spirit and a maverick charm that set him apart. Nothing seemed beyond his reach as he fearlessly embarked on a series of audacious heists, targeting ranches, trains, coaches, and even banks. The mere mention of his name sent shivers down the spines of those unfortunate enough to be caught in his path.

Antonio's audacious exploits not only transgressed the boundaries of societal norms but also left behind a visceral wave of fear that reverberated through the hearts of his victims. Whether it was the relentless pursuit of fortune or the love for the thrill of adventure. Bandit Antonio had evaded Marshal Chapman many times, the exact place they were resting, he was aware of the closeness to Whiteoak's he set up guards around the perimeter of the rocks. His day of reckoning was drawing closer the nights fire enhanced the whiskey fuelled conversations between the band of men.

Whiteoak's was only a few hours ride, As he sat around the crackling campfire, his loyal men by his side, his mind overflowed with a cascade of ideas and possibilities. The flickering flames mirrored the intensity within him, fuelling his determination. With each passing moment, he crafted a masterful blueprint for their grand assault, taking into account every nuisance and potential obstacle. Antonio's adventurous spirit embraced the thrill of the unknown, his revenge on Sheriff Smiff and Marshal Chapman was his only concern, He was to send two scouts to survey the town, if approached they were to ask to refresh and water their horses, the plan was to enter the town from the east side, past the wood yard and haberdashery at Belle end and ride through 2nd Street and take the town.

As the sun began to rise, the campfire extinguished, the group of men mounted their steeds and embarked on their murderous journey. The thundering sound of their hooves echoed through the land, Twenty riders rode hard as their faces filled with determination and a touch of wildness and ruggedness, a force to reckon with. The earth quivered beneath their powerful hooves, as if acknowledging the primal energy that pulsed through the air, With each thunderous beat, the riders dared to embrace the unknown and traverse uncharted territories. It was a moment frozen in time, where courage and adrenaline merged. They came to a halt just outside the town boundaries. The two scouts eager to start with their hearts pounding in excitement and a glimmer of anticipation in their eyes, the two scouts stood at the edge of the town, ready to embark on their daring mission and report back with valuable information back to Antonio. As the sun has just rose the towns people had no idea what was about to happen, they quietly when through their daily chores, an unexpected turn of events was about to unfold. Little did Antonio know, a sharp-eyed miner had witnessed the arrival of a group of mysterious riders, their presence shrouded in a cloak of secrecy. As the hazy silhouettes emerged from the shimmering heat and dust. Antonio and his bandits, with their bandoleers and wide-brimmed hats, stood against the backdrop of the blazing sun, a menacing sight.

Fuelling the flames of curiosity, the miner wasted no time in dashing towards the weathered office of Sheriff Smiff, envisioning his heroic role in bringing justice to the lawless frontier. As he burst through the creaking door, the miner's breathless words tumbled forth, revealing the imminent danger lurking just beyond the town's boundaries. Unbeknownst to Antonio, a tempest of action and thrills was about to descend upon them, setting the stage for an epic battle between honour and lawlessness.

The two scouts rode into town, their eyes taking in every detail of the bustling streets. As they entered the dusty thoroughfare, they had no idea what awaited them. Suddenly, out of nowhere, Sheriff Smiff stood before them, his imposing figure and stern gaze making it clear that he meant business. The scouts exchanged a quick glance before dismounting their horses, preparing for whatever challenge lay ahead.

"Hey Amigo, where can we water our horses and replenish ours?" the two scouts called out, their words carrying a persuasive tone of voice.

The weariness in their eyes and the dust on their trusted steeds spoke volumes of their journey through the arid land. In a firm and persuasive tone, Sheriff Smiff quickly responded, commanding the individuals to turn around and head back to where they came from. There was a sense of authority in his voice, leaving no room for negotiations or hesitation. It was clear that Sheriff Smiff was determined to enforce the law and order of the town. Marshal Chapman and the two Rangers were unwavering in their mission to protect the community from any potential threats or disruptions that loomed on the horizon. With the knowledge that a fight was imminent, Again Sheriff Smiff commanding the individuals to turn around and head back to where they came from. As the two Scouts turned they called out "Listen closely, for there is a dire warning that must not go unheard." With a grave conviction, they uttered words that sent shivers down spines and roused the deepest fears within all who heard. "Hell is coming," "Hell is coming," they proclaimed, their voices laced with an unwavering certainty, "and it will devour every soul within its path." Their persuasive tone carried the weight of truth, leaving no room for scepticism. In their ominous words, they painted a vivid picture of imminent peril towards the town.

As the tension heightened in Whiteoak's, the two scouts realized they were unwelcome and their cover was thwart, they swiftly pivoted their horses and galloped back the way they had come in. Their urgent departure conveyed a sense of purpose and urgency, Marshal Chapman and Sheriff Smiff skilfully herded a few townspeople In a daring display of resourcefulness, deftly manoeuvring them into position to create a formidable barricade. Working with precision and efficiency, they swiftly turned over a nearby wagon, cleverly utilizing its bulk to fortify their defence. With a calculated strength, they effortlessly lifted crates and sturdy pieces of wood and barrels, strategically arranging them to construct a solid barrier. Their actions exuded a confidence and fearlessness When the town's safety was on the line, the Marshal didn't hold back. With a voice that commanded attention and respect, Marshal Chapman called for other town members who possessed sharpshooting skills was nothing short of bold. The town was about to be plagued by lawlessness and was in peril, A few members answered the call, Mr Whiteoak the Gunsmith,

Mr Thomas the Bank manager, John Boxx from the Assay Office and many more, their guns trained on towards the barricade, they had at least plenty of supplies from the Gunsmith, Amidst the chaos, a courageous group of wives stood united, resolute, and prepared for whatever may come their way. The Marshal's wife and the Sheriff's wife stood ever vigilant, poised to provide swift medical aid to any wounded souls. The weight of waiting hung thick in the air, burdening their hearts with an undeniable sense of tension and fear that was about to embark on them.

The four lawmen stood tall and unwavering. The weight of responsibility rested on their shoulders, but they exuded a confidence that radiated throughout the crowd of anxious townspeople. There was an aura of anticipation hanging in the air, as if time stood still in anticipation of their command. The unknown awaited them, As the eastern side of the town was narrow, it proved to be an advantageous feat for both the townspeople and the lawmen responsible for defending it. As the anticipation hung in the air, the long-awaited moment finally arrived. Suddenly, just as predicted, the riders emerged from the east side. With their hulking frames and determined expressions, the twenty horsemen presented an ominous sight. Their presence evoked a sense of awe mixed with a tinge of trepidation, fuelling the burgeoning fear within, With their hearts pounding and adrenaline coursing through their veins, the four Lawmen stood tall, their voices firm and unwavering. Echoing across the town, their resolute call urged the intruders to swiftly reconsider their ill-fated path and turn around. The bandits continued to ride into town, their guns blazing, the Barricade stood tall and immovable, stopping them dead in their tracks. With an intrepid and adventurous spirit, the townspeople had prepared for this moment, constructing a formidable barrier to defend their homes and loved ones. As the dust settled, the bandits dismounted from their horses. With fearless determination radiating from his every pore, Marshal Chapman grasped the attention of towns folk and bellowed the commanding words that would ignite a thrilling chain of events: "Fire!" The air crackled with anticipation as the town's folks tightened their grips on their weapons, their hearts pounding, the crack of gun fire echoed loudly through the street, the fight had begun, adrenaline rushing through every vein, the Bandits had quickly taken cover, some terrified townsfolk, all seeking refuge of the battle. The deafening sound of gunfire reverberated through the air, echoing the bravery and audacity that fuelled this epic clash. Sweat dripped down their brows, mixing with the dirt and grime, as they fearlessly aimed and fired at each other, fully immersed in the relentless pursuit of victory. Amidst the frenzy, one audacious bandit seized the opportunity to wreak havoc, effortlessly flinging a fiery torch towards the helpless, upturned wagon trying to make a breakthrough, there emerged the figure of Franco. With nerves of steel and a spirit unyielding, he fearlessly charged towards the burning wreckage. Ignoring the showers of sparks, he single-handedly fought back the encroaching flames under heavy gunfire, Franco with his unwavering bravery, the wagon was ultimately extinguished, preventing further destruction.

The audacity and resolve they displayed left the Bandits pinned down, unable to move forward, the fight seemed to know no end, with an unyielding barrage of bullets being fired and weapons being diligently reloaded. Every moment appeared to be frozen in time, as if the universe itself had paused to witness the relentless clash. It was a sight that defied all reason, a spectacle of bravery or just madness, With each trigger pulled and every cartridge exchanged, a haunting symphony of horror echoed in the air. The unforgiving morning pressed on as the smoke gradually cleared, revealing the aftermath of this relentless battle. The bandits, overwhelmed by the magnitude of resistance, could do nothing but retreat to regroup. Marshal Chapman and Sheriff Smiff could see the aftermath, As several bandits had been killed and slumped over the barricade, The Marshall and Sheriff Smiff dusted off their clothes, they discovered that the extent of any town casualties but to their astonishment the injuries merely amounted to a few cuts and grazes. The pungent smell of burnt powder hung heavy in the air, a stark reminder of the intense battle that had taken place. Despite the acrid scent, a sense of triumph lingered. Although the initial count of bandit's ranks had dwindled from twenty men to a mere fifteen, deep within his resolute heart, he knew that Antonio, their fearless commander, would defy all odds and fight until the bitter end. With every setback only fuelled the fire burning within their souls.

With unwavering determination and boldness, the wives of the men in the town valiantly rushed to their loved ones' side, armed with water and ammunition to restock. These fearless women refused to be bystanders in the face of adversity. Their hearts filled with fierce loyalty, they stood ready to provide aid and support to their husbands, The Marshal's commanding voice cut through the thick tension, ringing in their ears with a stern authority. He bellowed for his comrades to hold their ground, his words echoing off the walls, fuelling their spirits. The atmosphere crackled with anticipation as the palpable tension reached new heights. Each townsmen tightened their grip on their weapons, their hearts pounding as they were ready. There was silence and birds could be heard in the distance, Then the preacher 'Mark' emerged from a corner of the town with an air of boldness, captivating the attention of all who laid eyes upon him.

His fiery gaze pierced through the crowd, leaving an indelible impression on their souls. John, a devout believer, was startled as he noticed his Bible firmly clasped in one hand, while the other held a pistol. In that moment, he couldn't help but feel a surge of gratitude. It was as if two conflicting forces were merging within him, representing the delicate balance between faith and protection. The peaceful silence that once enveloped the atmosphere was abruptly shattered by a resounding thunder of hooves. The bandits, who had previously vanished into the shadows, reappeared with an air of menace that seemed to bring forth a sense of hell itself, the battleground of Whiteoak's echoed with the screams of anguish and the clashing of weapons. The fight, ignited once more, The air was thick with smoke again the sound of gun fire echoed through the street, as veins filled with adrenaline, blurring the vision of even the most battle-hardened townsfolks and bandits. The siege of Whiteoak's was far from an ordinary conflict; it was a relentless struggle for survival and where courage was the only currency worth fighting for. Shot after shot as the noise was deafening, As gun smoke billowed into the air, engulfing the 2nd street, the pungent scent of burnt powder lingered, a testament to the intense firefight that had just taken place. Amidst the chaos, a sudden clearing appeared within the bandit ranks, revealing a figure that stood out among the rest. With a bold tone of voice, Mr. Whiteoak called out to Marshal Chapman, his words filled with confidence and triumph, as he declared, "I've got him!" The significance of this moment reverberated through the air, As the bullets whizzed through the air and the dust kicked up around them, the Marshal's sharp eyes caught sight of Antonio's wounded figure, Mr Whiteoak was right, Antonio with two of his loyal bandits with their unwavering commitment to survive another day and fight again fled, leaving the rest to uncertainty, most of them fled too, only three remained and soon dropped their weapons and held their hands high, The Two rangers quickly bound the men, it was time the townsfolk check for casualties what seemed another miracle only two had suffered minor gunshot wounds and Franco minor burns from the wagon and the wife's was quick to treat them.

The four lawmen breathed a collective sigh of relief as the siege came to an end. After hours of tension and fierce gunfire, victory was finally theirs. Overjoyed and filled with a sense of accomplishment, Tan, the Preacher's wife, wasted no time in announcing the great news. She hurriedly made her way to the church bell and rang it with resounding enthusiasm. The sound echoed through the town, carrying a message of triumph and hope for all to hear. It was a bold declaration that the danger had retreated, and peace could once again prevail.

The Marshal stood tall, his authoritative voice ringing through the air as he addressed the remaining townspeople. "We could have lost some of our own, but we cannot let fear consume us. We shall stand firm, unwavering in our commitment to protect this town." His words echoed with boldness, instilling a renewed sense of determination in the hearts of those listening. "Stay vigilant, my friends, for we do not know if any of them may return. Keep your eyes peeled, your senses sharp, and your weapons at the ready. Our strength lies in our unity and our unwavering bravery which is our town called Whiteoak's." After the Marshal said that, Tony, John, Smiff, Soapy and the Marshal headed towards the Saloon, they stood at the bar and all ordered a drink, "whiskey all round," The barkeeper placed the bottle before them, their eager expressions reflecting their shared camaraderie. Pouring a glass for each of them, they raised their drinks in unison, a toast to Whiteoak's with heartfelt cheer. Savouring the fiery liquid, they momentarily escaped into the warmth of the moment before resuming their regular routines.

The three bandits were sent to Fort Worth to the District Judge, After the recent events that befell our town, After leaving us under siege from relentless bandits, it was evident that we could no longer afford to ignore the devastation they had left in their wake. The time had come for us, the townspeople, to muster our collective strength and address the aftermath head-on. With an unwavering resolve, we devised a comprehensive plan to clear up the destruction that had befallen our once-thriving community. The townsfolk started to gradually regain a sense of normalcy in their lives. The resilience and determination of the community were truly remarkable. Day by day, the streets once filled with detritus and despair began to slowly transform into bustling hubs of activity once again. The local businesses, with doors once closed, started reopening, providing a glimmer of hope for the town's recovery. Mr J Boxx head of construction delegated a party of workers to repair buildings, the School house, the roof on the bank and the saddlery needed to be address first, while everyone else continued in their daily chores. Most of the town folks, driven by a fierce determination, wasted no time in clearing the detritus. With their sleeves rolled up and a steely resolve, they tackled the debris left behind, their minds sharply reminded of the harsh reality that comes with living in a frontier town. They knew all too well the unforgiving nature of their surroundings – if its unpredictable weather, the sporadic attacks from outlaws, or just the constant struggle for survival, they know that they have a sense of community. The Marshal deep down knew that

Bandit Antonio wouldn't rest until either one of them had been killed, but for now peace had been restored. It didn't take much time for Sheriff Smiff and Marshal Chapman to dust off their boots and jump right back into their daily duties.

These two law enforcement heroes didn't waste a moment before they were back on the streets, keeping the peace and serving justice with their trademark wit and charm, their eyes scanning the empty street ahead. With a touch of curiosity, they couldn't help but ponder what lurked around the corner. Perhaps another mischievous outlaw plotting their next heist or a curious traveller seeking adventure. Whatever it may be, these savvy lawmen were ready for anything, a twinkle of excitement in their eyes and a smirk hinting at the unpredictable future. After all, in this frontier town, one could never underestimate the surprises awaiting them just beyond the horizon.

End.

Chapter 15

Acknowledgements:

Author: Mr Andy M Chapman   *Illustrator: Mr. Ian Lyle*

Research: Wikipedia, Texas History and Whiteoak Springs Western Town.

Images: Courtesy of Town Members and Photographer Mr Dave Tomlinson.

Cover Image: Courtesy Mr Phil Powling.

Back Stories: Gratitude to those town members who contributed their own back story.

This book wouldn't be possible if it wasn't for everyone at Whiteoak's their unwavering commitment, passion, every weekend of gatherings and roundups which has shaped this literary gem into what it is today. From the editor who sculpted words to the illustrator who created visual magic, each individual's contribution is priceless. This is an incredible team at Whiteoak's, and has demonstrated their experience, expertise, authority, and trust, which elevates this book to extraordinary heights. This was a grand gesture from Tom and his family and without his commitment for letting Tony build Whiteoak's Springs many of us wouldn't be continuing with the hobby.

Printed in Great Britain
by Amazon